by Joyce Carol Oates

Novels
With Shuddering Fall (1964)
A Garden of Earthly Delights (1967)
Expensive People (1968)
Them (1969)
Wonderland (1971)
Do With Me What You Will (1973)

Stories
By the North Gate (1963)
Upon the Sweeping Flood (1966)
The Wheel of Love (1970)
Marriages and Infidelities (1972)

Poetry
Women In Love (1968)
Anonymous Sins (1969)
Love and Its Derangements (1970)
Angel Fire (1973)
Dreaming America (1973)

Criticism
The Edge of Impossibility (1972)
The Hostile Sun: the Poetry of D. H. Lawrence (1973)

Editor
Scenes From American Life (1973)

JOYCE
CAROL
OATES

The Hungry Ghosts

SEVEN
ALLUSIVE
COMEDIES

Black Sparrow Press • *Los Angeles* • *1974*

ACKNOWLEDGEMENTS: "Democracy in America" was originally published in *Shenandoah* (Spring 1973). "Pilgrims' Progress" (titled "Saul Bird Says: Relate! Communicate! Liberate!") was originally published in *Playboy* (Oct. 1970), and received 2nd Prize in the *O. Henry Awards* for 1972. "Up From Slavery" (titled "The Loves of Franklin Ambrose") was published in *Playboy* (Jan. 1972).
"A Descriptive Catalogue" was published in *Carolina Quarterly* (Fall 1973). "The Birth of Tragedy" was published in *Exile* (Winter 1974). "Angst" was published in *Windsor Review* (Spring 1974).

LIBRARY OF CONGRESS CATALOGING IN PUBLICATION DATA
Oates, Joyce Carol, 1938-
  The hungry ghosts.
  CONTENTS: Democracy in America.—Pilgrims' progress.
—Up from slavery. [etc.]
  I. Title.
PZ4.0122Hu [PS3565.A8]   813'.5'4   74-2272
ISBN 0-87685-204-5
ISBN 0-87685-203-7 (pbk.)
ISBN 0-87685-205-3 (signed, cloth)

—for those fictitious and ghostly colleagues whose souls haunt this book—

"A *preta* (ghost) is one who, in the ancient Buddhist cosmology, haunts the earth's surface, continually driven by hunger— that is, desire of one kind or another."

CONTENTS

Satire is a sort of Glass, wherein Beholders do generally
discover everybody's Face but their Own. . . .

Jonathan Swift, *The Battle of the Books*

. . Surely a man may speak truth with a smiling countenance.

Henry Fielding, *Tom Jones*

DEMOCRACY IN AMERICA

He scanned the list of names by the mail slots, saw that name *Dietrich* and ignored it, and pressed the button beside the name *Novak*. It was Dr. Novak's wife he was supposed to contact. No response. For the fourth or fifth time in the last several minutes he checked his watch—it was 10:30 now, time for their meeting. He had taken a bus across town and, as usual, had started out far too early, so that he arrived at the Novaks' apartment building twenty minutes ahead of time. A nervous habit of his, left over from his student days; horribly, *he was always early for everything*. In spite of the drizzle he had walked around the block several times. Now he was wet, selfconscious, already a little intimidated by Mrs. Novak. He pressed the white plastic button again and this time, thank God, a loud buzzer sounded and the lock to the heavy front door was released. A small female voice said, "Come in. . . ." without requiring him to identify himself. He seized the oversized brass doorknob and shoved the door open. Yet still the voice spoke to him out of a device overhead, as if doubting his ability to maneuver himself into the foyer, "Come in . . . come in, please. . . ."

The foyer smelled of aged, worn-down, dust-weighted carpeting, though he could see that it was an Oriental rug and had once been opulent. Opulent too, and slightly tarnished, were the brass fixtures and wall-lights and the unlighted chandelier. No one was around, so he walked quickly to the stairway, hoping to get up there before

11

Mrs. Novak came down to meet him. He didn't want much personal contact with her; that would just be interpreted as a strategy on his part, to gain favor with her husband. Anyway he intended to get this over as quickly as possible. He hoped to be back in his own apartment by 11:30. Classes began on Monday at the University and he was anxious to prepare his work, his introductory lectures; it was only his second year at this university and he was not exactly certain of his future.

Upstairs, the door to the first apartment on the right was open, and Ronald heard someone talking inside. Then a woman appeared —a short, darkhaired woman—and said, "Mr. Pauli . . .? I'm Ingrid Novak."

"Ronald," he said. It came out awkwardly. He was a little surprised at Mrs. Novak's appearance: she was younger than he had imagined, and she wore maroon slacks and a sweater or jersey blouse that seemed to be made of strands of bright contrasting color, red and a glinting magenta, threaded through with a silkish red-blue. He tried to smile and respond in a friendly, attentive manner as she asked him how he was, wasn't it a shame about the rain and the floods along the lake, and would he like to come inside for coffee or tea first . . . ? Though she was about his age, in her early thirties, she spoke to him in a kindly maternal way. For some reason this made him very nervous. "I really don't have much time," he said. "The next few days are going to be very busy for me, and. . . ."

A child called out. Mrs. Novak said over her shoulder, "Nothing, honey, nothing that concerns you," but to Ronald's dismay a little girl ran out anyway, to to stare up at him with a bright impudent smile. Of course, this necessitated Mrs. Novak's introducing him to "Janey," who was seven years old, and Ronald had to stand stiffly while the child seemed to be inspecting him; he had always disliked children, being an only child himself. The Novaks' little girl had curly light brown hair and kept asking her mother if she could come along with them downstairs. "I know where you're going," she said to Ronald.

"Of course you can't come along," Mrs. Novak said, pretending to be surprised. Then she insisted that Ronald hang up his raincoat in their foyer, and leave his briefcase up here. "There won't be any place you can put it down there," she said, and Ronald wondered what on earth was she talking about. But he gave in, trying to smile, as if he were not miserable to get away from Mrs. Novak's bright, rather insouciant manner.

Then she led him back downstairs, and down another flight of stairs to the basement. She held a key between her fingers and gestured with it as she spoke: it was a newly-stamped key, bright and cheaply shining. "Actually, I wanted to prepare you for Mr. Dietrich's room," she said apologetically. "I thought we could have coffee and talk first. . . . What did they tell you in the department office?"

Ronald almost slipped on the stairs. "What—what did they tell me?" He stared at the side of Mrs. Novak's face. "Why, they said that the copy-editor had died . . . that my manuscript was mixed up with his papers and I should come over here and get it. . . . What's wrong? Is the manuscript destroyed? Isn't it in his room?"

Down here, the light was ghastly and did not show Mrs. Novak to good effect. Her red-and-magenta outfit looked like a costume. She glanced at him, she hesitated before replying. "I'm sure it's in his room, Mr. Pauli, don't be upset," she said. "But it may take you a while to find it."

". . . to find it?" Ronald asked weakly.

There was only one apartment occupied in the basement, Mrs. Novak explained, now that Mr. Dietrich had died; the landlord wanted to close that apartment off or use it as a storage room, but the occupant—a senior nurse at the university hospital—refused to move. "Mr. Dietrich had rented this room for eight years, evidently," Mrs. Novak said, "ever since he came to town. Now don't be upset, please, because I'm sure your manuscript is safe . . . there's no evidence that he destroyed anything."

She unlocked the door and snapped on the light.

Ronald followed her in. What an odor!—and what a sight! He started. The room was a jumble of chairs, boxes, bedding, books, magazines, and stray papers. There was only one window, looking

1 3

out onto a window-well; its ancient shade was cracked in several places. Everywhere there was debris—empty tin cans, empty milk cartons and frozen food packages. The smell in the room made Ronald's eyes water, it was so sharp and acrid. He looked at the clutter for several long moments, in silence. He had never anticipated anything like this.

"What happened in here?" he asked Mrs. Novak finally.

"This is the way he left his room," she said.

"He lived here?—in this? Dietrich lived in *this*?"

"He was found dead here, you know," she said.

Ronald knew the man had been *found dead*, but he had not thought much about it. He had had time to think only about his manuscript. Now he stepped into the room slowly, drawing his fingers through his hair, feeling the pressure of his fingertips on his scalp. No. No, he couldn't believe it. All those papers scattered around—mixed in with garbage, with soiled clothing and bedding, crumpled beneath plates on which food had dried—"No," he said aloud, feeling sick. "I can't believe it. The copy-editor for the press —this Mr. Dietrich—he left things like this? *Like this?* He lived down here *like this*?"

Mrs. Novak remained in the doorway, silent. Ronald looked wildly back at her. She was trying to smile, to soften the horror. "The landlord refuses to do anything until the insurance adjustor is in," she said. "I knew what it was like because Mr. Dietrich's mother requested a few things, and I volunteered to look for them the other day. . . . I was down here this morning, earlier, and tried to get that window open so it wouldn't be too awful for you, but I couldn't budge it. The sill is warped."

"I'll open it," Ronald said, gagging. He stepped over some of the junk, but put his foot down on the rim of a plate; it broke in two. He strained to get the window up. He shifted his grip and pushed, but had no luck. He was becoming nauseated. Mrs. Novak came to help him, tugging from the bottom. After a few seconds' struggle they managed to get the window up two or three inches. Unable to stop himself, Ronald ducked and put his mouth into the space, breathing noisily, sucking in the fresh damp air as if he

14

were suffocating. He was ashamed of his desperation, and feared looking up at Mrs. Novak. He breathed deeply, his eyes closed.

"Evidently they didn't explain to you the circumstances . . . the circumstances of his death," she said. She was looking down at him with an odd, tender pity, and the emotion in her voice made him recover at once. *He didn't want pity.* "He was found dead. The place was like this, just the way it is now . . . he was lying in bed, he'd been in here for six or seven days. He died of natural causes. They did an autopsy. The secretaries at the office should have prepared you for this . . . I talked to one of them over the phone, and I asked my husband to talk to them, because . . . I felt very sorry for you, when I heard about your manuscript. That you didn't have a carbon copy. . . ."

Ronald stared at the debris. *If there should be cockroaches!* He didn't think he could bear that. He took a tissue out of his pocket, hurriedly, and blew his nose. His eyes were watering. He wiped his eyes, ashamed that Mrs. Novak should be watching him. Looking over the room he couldn't seem to focus on anything—couldn't locate any clear space. It was all a jumble, a tumult of overturned things, clothes and sheets and towels that seemed to have been twisted together, in rage. Then, he saw that the room had a kind of logic to it: a kitchen area at one end, with a pullman refrigerator, a table piled with junk, and a hot plate on the sink, all of this partly concealed by a screen that had been tipped back toward the wall; in the dim light from the overhead bulb, this screen glimmered a pale, luminous yellow, and the outline of a woman's figure seemed to be painted on it. Next was an enormous desk, piled with junk, including a desk lamp with a broad metallic base, just like the one Ronald had on his own desk, and an aluminum towel rack that had been tossed down. A pillow case hanging from one of the bars. On the swivel chair before the desk was a pair of dark trousers, with a belt hanging loose and unbuckled, and some underwear, and a small stack of newspapers. There was an unusual amount of furniture for so small a room—an old-fashioned bureau with its drawers partly yanked out, two easy chairs, a straight-back chair lying on its side, a floor lamp with a large scalloped lamp-

15

shade. Everywhere there were books and magazines and papers, as if blown back and forth across the room by a mad wind, coming to rest in corners, beneath pieces of furniture, on top of dirty dishes. Ronald wanted to laugh, it was so horrible. Everything lay under a kind of spell, weighted-down, cold, horrible. And the odor!. . . . It was not one odor but many. He could almost see the promiscuous swirls of separate odors, rising like fumes from tin cans, from tea-bags and crusts of bread and dirty socks. . . . Beneath his foot was a typewritten page. He saw that it was stained with dried juice from a tuna fish can that had been tossed onto it. "How could he . . . how could anyone live like this?" Ronald asked softly.

"His mother is in a nursing home in Boston, and she wanted someone to find a few things for her," Mrs. Novak said, slowly. "So I . . . I volunteered. Someone had to do it. I sifted through some of the papers on his desk and in the drawers, and found a few photographs to send her, but then I had to leave. I couldn't take it. . . . Is it an entire manuscript you're looking for? A book-length manuscript?"

"Three hundred eighty-five pages," Ronald said. He walked care-fully across the room, following a kind of path through the junk. He could even see the imprint of someone's foot, in a pile of sheets. He opened a closet door. There was another door beside it, but when he reached for the doorknob Mrs. Novak said sharply, "No, don't—"

"What's wrong?"

"That's the bathroom," she said. "It's very dirty."

Ronald hesitated.

"Don't open the door, please," she said.

Ronald tried to turn without knocking anything over. He felt lightheaded, almost giddy. Across the way was another door. "Is that another closet?" he asked.

"No, it's one of those you pull down from the wall. It was his bed," Mrs. Novak said.

Ronald shuddered. "There aren't any papers in there, then . . . ?"

"No. I don't think so."

He waded through trash and peered into the closet. Strangely, there wasn't much in the closet—a half-dozen items of clothing on hangers, pushed far to the right as if someone had angrily shoved them there. On a shelf were some rumpled shirts and more socks. On the floor, two pairs of men's shoes, both black, and a pillow without a pillowcase, made of a very white foam rubber. Ronald moved the pillow with his foot and saw, beneath it, a typewritten page. He bent over to read it, not wanting to pick it up.

> . . . the failure of Rogers' analysis of the 'formula' of Tocqueville's methodology can be related to the one-sided emphasis of Heinemann in *Beard and Tocqueville*,[23] which seems also to have influenced. . . .

"I found a page," he said bleakly.

". . . from your book?"

"Yes." Ronald stooped to pick it up, swaying. He had difficulty getting hold of it. Mrs. Novak came over to his side, and he felt his brain dissolve—black out—then in the next instant he was straightening again and showing the page to Mrs. Novak, as if nothing had happened and he were normal. He felt a sickish, uncontrollable grin about to distort his face. To forestall it he raised his fist to his mouth and rubbed his dry lips roughly; the sensation seemed numb, distant, as if it belonged to another person. Mrs. Novak appeared to be reading the page, though the lighting was poor and she had to stand with it raised awkwardly. "Don't bother reading it," Ronald said, embarrassed. "You wouldn't find it interesting . . . it isn't meant to be interesting. . . . It's a complete survey of twentieth-century criticism of the works of Tocqueville and Grattan. Mr. Dietrich was supposed to check some of the references. They told me at the Press when the book was accepted that they always had part-time help do this kind of copy-editing, even though I said I could do it myself. But they said that wasn't their policy. They said this Dietrich was reliable! . . . My God, what am I going to do?" he said bitterly. "First I had that incident with my luggage lost, and the valise with the carbon copy in it never located . . . then I get back to town here and they tell me that there's been a slight problem, that someone I never heard of before, someone they trusted my manuscript with, was found dead . . . he was *found dead* . . . and I asked Dr. Mercer what the problem was, but Dr. Mercer said the man had died of natural causes and there wasn't any problem, as far as he knew, but that I should talk to one of the secretaries. My life has become so confused. . . ." He noticed that Mrs. Novak was no longer reading the page, but looking toward him, not quite at him, as if waiting for him to finish. She was strangely passive, polite; yet he realized suddenly that she wanted to escape. They were standing quite close together. Beyond them, around them, threatening them was the ill-lit room with its raging stink. Ronald wanted to seize her and beg for help, for mercy, for understanding. "Did you and your husband know Mr. Dietrich well? he asked.

"I saw him occasionally, getting his mail," Mrs. Novak said. She spoke in a slow, reluctant voice. "No one knew him well. He didn't have any friends . . . no one came to his funeral. His mother is evidently his only surviving relative, and she's an invalid. We didn't know him at all. Once I ran into him at Kroger's and tried to talk to him, just to ask how he was, but I got the impression that Janey made him nervous . . . Janey was with me . . . or maybe he was just shy, I don't know."

She handed him the page. Ronald knew she would be leaving now, and he resented it; he felt in a way that she was to blame for this; *someone was to blame.* "They assured me that this 'Mr. Dietrich' was reliable!" he said angrily. ". . . What did he look like?"

"He wore glasses with thick lenses," Mrs. Novak said, reluctantly. "I don't think I ever looked at him, exactly. I mean closely. He wasn't the kind of man you felt that comfortable with. . . . He was tall and thin and seemed nervous, always moving his hands. They kept him on in the history department for years, as a part-time instructor, even though Dr. Mercer got complaints from his students—he wasn't a very good teacher, he was old-fashioned, he didn't like his students. Or maybe he was afraid of them. The extension division had to channel students into his section of Democracy 100, but they just didn't like him. It was a hopeless situation.

18

Then . . . well . . . the budget was cut and most of the night-school courses were dropped, so they decided to non-renew Mr. Dietrich; that was in the spring quarter, last year. But the university press hired him for short-term projects, like your book."

Ronald laughed bitterly.

"He wasn't that bad!" Mrs. Novak said. "Something must have happened to him over the summer. . . . I saw him two or three times, and he looked so strange . . . he looked almost white, almost blood-less . . . he would say *Hello, Mrs. Novak!* in an ironic way, as if there were a joke between us, or a joke about something I didn't understand. But I didn't know him at all. I didn't think about him at all. I felt that he hated me, and he certainly hated my husband. It was a hopeless situation. . . ."

She stepped through the rubble, with a fastidious, somehow practiced grace, and again Ronald had the impulse to grab hold of her. She was such a pretty woman, even in this place! He was think-ing that something was unfair, something was viciously, crazily un-fair, and she was going to walk away from it. She was going to escape. Ronald burst out: "It's almost as if this all happened on purpose. My carbon copy of the book was stolen at the airport. Someone had made off with it, and why?—what would anyone want with it? My luggage was put on the wrong plane, and when it finally got to me the valise with the manuscript was miss-ing, *of course*, and all they can tell me at the airline office is that they're sorry. And whoever stole the valise, obviously he took one look inside at my papers and books and threw it all away! It had no value to *him*! The bastard! . . . I'm sorry to talk like this," he said; he was suddenly struck by the tone of his loud, whining voice. Mrs. Novak looked back at him, pityingly. He felt he must explain. "I realize it wasn't Mr. Dietrich's fault that he died, I realize it was a tragic thing. . . . But I've been very upset about many things, it wasn't certain until the middle of the summer whether I still had a job here . . . thanks to Dr. Mercer finally things got straightened out, but . . . but still I've been upset. My life seems so haphazard. Having my book accepted by the Press was the one certain thing, the one reality . . . and Dr. Mercer said he was sure I'd be kept on, he was sure the Department's executive committee would be impressed with it, my having a book accepted. It means so much to me. . . . And now this, this crazy mess. . . ." He stared at Mrs. Novak. Then, for some reason, he asked suddenly: "How old was he?—Dietrich?"

"Thirty-nine."

"*What?*"

"Thirty-nine."

Ronald could not believe he had heard correctly. "A . . . a thirty-nine-year-old man was found dead? . . . just *found dead?*"

Mrs. Novak colored slightly. She hesitated; Ronald had the impression that she was about to protest that it hadn't been her fault. But she said, evenly, "An autopsy was ordered, but the coroner said he died of natural causes. He died. He just died. He just . . . died."

"And he was in here a week?"

"I think so, yes."

Mrs. Novak tried to smile at him. He could not be certain if it was a friendly smile, or an ironic smile; if she liked him or was already rehearsing in her mind the anecdote she would tell her husband about him, Ronald Pauli, standing there in befuddlement, quivering with disgust and terror, a single page of his manuscript in hand—page 112—and three hundred eighty-four yet to be found. Her complexion was slightly flushed, her dark eyes, level, yet remote and passive, as if she were already gone from him, hurrying upstairs to the safety of the second floor, putting him out of her mind. But she waited politely while he apologized again for his outburst, and thanked her again for being so generous; and she told him that she would be taking her daughter to school at about twelve-thirty—"They're on half-session, the public schools are nearly bankrupt in this city!"—and that if he wanted to come upstairs for lunch, or just to rest, he was certainly welcome.

No, he just couldn't decide: did she like him, or was she secretly laughing at him?

As soon as she left he felt an odd, perverse relief. Now he could be alone, unobserved. Now he would not have to share this em-

barrassing odor with anyone. He took out his crumpled tissue again
and wiped his face, and then stood for several minutes without
moving, without even thinking. *Thirty-nine years old!* Then, wak-
ing, he went at once over to the desk. It was a large battered desk
with an old-fashioned sliding top, and its pigeon holes were stuffed
with papers and strange items—several old, dirty toothbrushes,
which had evidently been used to clean something, a container of
Black Paw shoe polish, a spool on which just a little white thread
remained, even a crumpled bag that had onceheld potato chips.
Ronald had to fight the impulse to cry out in vexation. He forced
himself to sit quietly at the desk, in the swivel chair, and to go
through the drawers in a sane, methodical manner. Fortunately he
was in a line of fresh air from the window; he instructed himself to
take deep, slow, intelligent breaths. He found several pages from
his manuscript almost immediately. Then he came upon part of
what must have been someone else's manuscript—consisting of
pages 11 through 39—and a curious item: a mimeographed notice
for a picnic held on June 15, 1971. *Come One Come All Poli Sci
Dept Picnic Glasberg Lake BYOB.* Someone had doodled on the
notice, in ballpoint pen. Ronald looked more closely: it wasn't
doodling but drawing, a clumsy, faint, feathery drawing of what
looked like a lake and some clouds.

Despair rose about him, like fumes. Ronald stuffed the notice
back into a drawer.

Another two pages of his manuscript were mixed up with university newsletters and forms having to do with insurance and hos-
pitalization programs, and Ronald cleared a space on top of the
desk for his manuscript. *He was going to find it all.* He came across
some books that turned out to be library books, due August 29. It
was now September 9. He put them carefully off to the side, thinking that he would take them back to the library himself, but in the
next instant he forgot about them in his excitement over locating
another half-dozen pages of his book. He glanced through them,
and found himself reading about Tocqueville's analysis of the
"natural inclination of democratic peoples to political and eco-
nomic conservatism" and only gradually, uneasily, did he come to

think that this wasn't his writing. . . . No, it wasn't his; he had been fooled because the type resembled his own. But it obviously belong to someone else's manuscript. Though he had no time to waste, he couldn't resist glancing through the pages . . . he felt a strange light-headedness, a bewilderment tinged with envy. . . . Whoever had written these pages seemed much more confident of his argument than Ronald had been; his own writing now stuck him as weak and tentative. But he gathered these papers together with those evidently belonging to other, separate manuscripts, and put them in a pile off to one side. He wondered if they belonged to other young men, like himself, who were anxious to do well . . . rivals who were not in this room to compete with him, but whose invisible forms swayed and lunged around him.

To offset his feeling of despair he began to work faster. He overturned one of the desk drawers to make sure everything was out—a cascade of papers, letters, pencil stubs, paper clips, a typewriter ribbon that fell out of its plastic case and rolled across his feet, unraveling as if it were alive—and immediately regretted it, making such a mess. He had to calm down. He forced himself to sift through the pages he had gathered so far of his manuscript, and to put them in order. He discovered that he had about seventy-five pages altogether, beginning with page 3. Most were stained or ripped a little but he tried not to let this upset him.

When he left the relative stability of the desk, he noticed at once how odors rose as if springing into life—he had only to lift an item of junk to release some ugly acrid knife-like smell. Thank God for the window, and for the occasional fresh air! It was still raining softly, a steady drizzling murmur, and Ronald absent-mindedly stared at the window for a few seconds thinking that he was looking out at the sky—a vague seamless featureless blur of gray—until he realized that he was in a basement apartment and was looking out at a window-well. It reminded him of the horrible eight months he had spent once in a basement apartment in New Brunswick, when he had been a graduate student at Rutgers. . . . But he had to keep going, had to get this task finished. Even Dietrich's soiled, bunched-together underwear and socks could not kep him from finding his pages . . . he kicked them aside, and there, yes there, were some typewritten pages that looked like his . . . he scanned the top page, page 118, and read of *a comprehension that is almost mathematical in its rigor, its unrhetorical unstrained, unlyric analysis of the manifold directions social democracy must take. . . .* When he leafed through his pile of manuscript pages, however, he saw that he already had a page 118. So this did belong to someone else.

He forgot about stacking these pages with the others, the rivals' work, and absent-mindedly stuffed them in a drawer. His method was too haphazard. He must begin again, more logically. It would make sense to move slowly from one end of the room to the other, step by step, inch by inch, in order to cover every conceivable square foot of space and to fight panic. Yet he could not help seeing corners of pages, crumpled balls that might have been pages, and his immediate impulse was to stoop to investigate. It was a shock to come across many pages from the local telephone directory, simply torn out and scattered . . . why on earth would anyone rip pages out of the telephone directory? Bemused, Ronald counted seven, eight, nine . . . twelve pages that had been ripped out and were mixed in with off-prints of essays published by the *Journal of American and Canadian Studies,* the scholarly quarterly that was edited at this university, and other items, stray and promiscuous. Ronald moved along in a squatting position, his thighs aching, for some time. Then he lifted a batch of mimeographed papers and saw a pile of plates with food dried on them—and a scurrying of insects—and at once he jumped to his feet, crying out in alarm. *Cockroaches!* He was almost overcome with nausea. He stumbled to the window and bent to get fresh air, tasted vomit at the back of his mouth, and in a sudden maniacal terror he yanked the window up another six inches. He knelt and thrust his head out into the window-well. Thank God, thank God . . . rain pelted his face, merciless cold antiseptic tear-drops. . . .

". . . Mr. Pauli?"

He scrambled back inside, and saw Mrs. Novak in the doorway.

"I was just checking to see how you were," she said, embarrassed.

"Fine. Just fine," Ronald stammered.

"Janey is at school now . . . so if you'd like any help. . . ."

Ronald was brushing at his trousers—they were dusty—he discovered they were very very dusty—and he wondered in anguish if his face was dirty—he couldn't remember if he had touched it— He was miserable, with this woman watching him from the doorway. How embarrassing that she had seen him at the window, kneeling like that, gasping for air helplessly!—he almost hated her. But he thanked her for her offer as if nothing were wrong. He told her that he was doing fine, that it wouldn't take much longer. She didn't look convinced, but said nothing. Ronald saw that she was an attractive woman, with an ache he saw how remote she was from him though she was actually standing a few yards away—and at her feet were a spillage of papers and several empty tin cans— the corners of his eyes ached, to see her there, observing him. *This is not really Ronald Pauli*, he wanted to cry. He brushed at his face and forehead with the back of his hand, which was clean. She invited him up for lunch, and he declined, nervously, miserably, noting her look of relief—or was it relief?—and finally she left him alone again.

"It won't take much longer," he repeated under his breath.

Now he did work feverishly. He moved along on his haunches, grunting with the effort. He set aside chairs, boxes, even pushing a heavy bureau aside with his shoulder, he discovered an old manual typewriter with its ribbon hopelessly snarled, and nearby was a batch of pages from his book—thirty-four pages! He exclaimed in delight. He tried to stand but his knees ached violently; he had to lean against the bureau for a few seconds, to regain his strength. When he re-examined his manuscript, now, he saw that he had about 250 pages so far . . . the first page was still page 3, and the last page was page 276.

And these pages were all his.

He felt so greedy, suddenly he had an idea—he ran over to the bathroom and opened the door. But the stench was too much for him. He slammed the door. He made his way back to the other end of the room, grimly, knowing that sanity consisted in his moving

24

methodically from one end to the other; he could not hope to conquer this chaos by jumping around wildly, trusting his impulses. —What an odor from that bathroom! What a filthy pig, a filthy degenerate pig, that Dietrich had been! Yet his stomach was miraculously calm; he half-expected a fit of gagging, but nothing happened. . . . He went back to work, stooping and picking through the trash, and when he glanced at his watch he saw in amazement that it was quarter to two. He wiped at his face with both hands. He stood, to clear his head, and surveyed the room as it lay before him: And he seemed to sense, or to actually see, the spectre of another man, a stranger, moving at the far end of the room, not bothering to step fastidiously over the debris but shuffling through it, leaden and indifferent. He was tall, thin, he was gesticulating to himself as if arguing. . . . It was as if the various fleeting bits of particles in the dim, dreary room for a moment coalesced into a form, and then in the next moment dissolved again.

Ronald rubbed his eyes.

Back to work! From time to time he was disturbed by footsteps overhead, and could not help remembering that squalid basement "apartment" of his back in New Jersey. A man and his wife had lived above him: the man heavy-footed, the woman disabled and required to use crutches. They had almost driven Ronald mad. . . . He found himself staring up at the ceiling here with a small furious paralyzed grin. He wondered if Dietrich, too, had sometimes paused to stare up at the ceiling. But the footsteps quieted and Ronald sifted through clothing and tossed it aside and came to the section of the wall he had thought to be a closet, but which was evidently a bed. Dietrich's death-bed. . . . He wondered if he should pull it down . . . ? Mrs. Novak had cautioned him against it, but she wasn't here . . . and she did not have the interest in Ronald's manuscript that he did, she couldn't be expected to understand how important it was to him. It was possible that a few papers were in there, hidden in there. He knew he should not pull it down, but . . . what if a few pages were in there? He stood there, rubbing his hands together, agitated, excited. *What if, what if . . . ?* Finally he grabbed at the two handles and pulled it down. He tried to pull it down slowly, but it was quite heavy, and the spring mechanism didn't work right, so he had to let it fall and leap back out of the way, so that it wouldn't break his toes. What a creaking, what a thud! for a horrible half-second he believed the entire building would resound with it, and people on every floor would know what he had done. But nothing happened. Everything was still except for the steady trickle of rain by the window.

It was a narrow bed. The bedclothes were still on it, ordinary white sheets that had turned a little yellow from many launderings, twisted together with a blanket of jade-green wool that looked fairly new. Ronald stared at all this. Then slowly, slowly, he pulled the top covers back so that he could look at the bottom sheet. . . . His heart pounding, he was able to make out after a while a dim pattern there, stiffened yellowish-white stains . . . .

Suddenly he felt faint. He stooped to get the bed up again, desperately, before someone came in and discovered him. But it was quite heavy. The spring on the left-hand side broke with a sharp, almost musical cry, and Ronald had to crawl under the bed in order to lift it, with the sheer strength of his back and shoulders. His brain swirled with panic and disgust. There was a moment when he thought that all was lost, that his mind would collapse completely and that there would be nothing left in this room but junk and that sound of trickling water, but he did not allow himself to surrender, he bit his lip and managed to get into a kneeling position, then into a squatting position. . . . Then in a final burst of strength he straightened and got the bed up into the wall.

He stepped cautiously away from it—but it held.

My God. . . .

Beneath a quilt were more manuscript pages—he pawed through them and believed they were his own—and he caught sight of more pages halfway beneath a lamp-stand, so he crawled forward and tilted it, but the base was quite heavy. This was an old-fashioned floor lamp with a columnar base, made of what looked like gray marble. The shaft of the column was fixed to the base, but the upper part—the electrical part of the lamp itself—was evidently balanced on the column. It fell with a crash. Ronald retrieved the pages, blowing dust and strands of cobwebs away. Though he was panting and felt over-heated, as if fevered, he took time to glance fondly through what he had written. He remembered typing this section of his book over, and over, revising it several times; originally, it had been a paper for a seminar at Rutgers, many years ago. He had received an *A* for it. He had written it somehow knowing, *knowing*, that it was going to receive an *A*. The last page of the bunch was very wrinkled; he tried to straighten it out, smoothing it against his leg, and he read: *The love of wealth is therefore to be traced, either as a principal or an accessory motive, at the bottom of all the Americans do: this gives to their passions a sort of family likeness, and soon renders the survey of them exceedingly wearisome. . . .*

But this quotation was from someone else's manuscript, as he saw now when he examined the type, so he let it fall. He didn't have time to retrieve other people's books.

When he added these pages to the pile on the desk, he saw that he had most of the book now. He slapped at his trousers, which were dusty, and turned to survey the room again. He felt much better. He was not so panicked, the stench did not bother him so much; it looked as if there weren't many pages still missing. This might have a happy ending after all. Feeling suddenly generous, Ronald righted the partition that screened the little kitchen area from the rest of the room, and saw that it was not really high enough to make much difference. It was made of pale yellow material that might have been silk. In the foreground was the stylized figure of a long-faced, slant-eyed Oriental woman, in the background a small stone bridge arching over a stream that was no more than a few brush strokes. The corners of the screen were smudged, from being handled, but otherwise it was in fairly good condition.

In his frantic hunting Ronald had kicked clothing around, and he regretted it now—he half-wondered if he should put things in a pile, if maybe he should go over the room again and try to straighten it up. And those loose papers belonging to other manuscripts. . . . It was absurd to feel guilty about them. And to worry about the heap of clothing: those food-stained trousers and cheap tweed suit-coats. When the room was cleaned all these things would be thrown away. Still, he picked up a sweater, and took a while to unknot its sleeves—for some reason its sleeves had been knotted tightly to-gether, as if in anger—and saw in surprise that it was made of good wool, in fact the label said *Cashmere Made in Scotland for Rowe, Burlington Arcade, London.* He hoped someday to get to London, himself . . . He held the sweater up against his chest, smoothed it down, and contemplated it, absent-mindedly. There was a large stain at the waist and he picked at it with his fingernails. . . . But what was he doing! He laughed nervously and laid the sweater on top of the bureau.

No, it was hopeless. This place could not be cleaned up. It would require hours of back-breaking labor, good hot scalding water, cleanser, disinfectant, a maniacal energy that could ignore the filth everywhere and not be nauseated by the food sticking to plates and the circus of smells. . . . Ronald could never do it. It was absurd to thing about it. Something sharp edged into his mind, a piercing un-easiness, a sense that there was something unfair about all this. . . . And his manuscript wasn't complete yet. Pages were still missing. What if he couldn't rewrite them? What if he had lost his ability to write? A horrible thought flashed to him: What if he were losing his mind?—*had already lost it*? What if he had spent all these hours putting together the manuscript of another man, and he him-self, Ronald Pauli, would be displaced? . . . He felt something nudge him from behind, and he jerked around. But it was only the doorknob of the bathroom door. On an impulse, eagerly, he opened the door again and held his breath, and this time snapped on the light. *Good God.* . . . His vision blotched. But he did make out, stacked loosely in the bathtub, more magazines and papers . . . the cover of an issue of the *Journal of American and Canadian Studies* . . . and more typewritten pages. . . . If he could just get over there. . . . If he could just snatch up an armful of those things. . . . He tried to avert his eyes from the filth. He took a deep breath before venturing in and held his chest as rigid as possible, but just as he stooped over to get the things in the bathtub he was forced to take a breath, and the odor almost made him faint. . . . But he wouldn't fail now. He seized the papers, let the magazines fall back into the dirt, and slammed the bathroom door. Hungrily, desperately, he leafed through the typewritten pages and saw—yes—yes, they were his—they were all his—*they were all his.*

In a frenzy of triumph he added them to the pile and slipped them in place, here were the missing pages, here everything was at last! All these pages were *his.* He tried not to notice the rips and dog-eared corners and the stains and smears of dust and dirt. Someone had tried to destroy him, but had not succeeded. His manuscript was crumpled, torn, stained with the dirt of a total stranger, but it had not been destroyed. And he had not been destroyed.

"I'm still living," Ronald whispered.

He went to the door. Everything was silent except for the rain. It must have been quite late—his watch had stopped at twenty minutes to five—and he felt light-headed from not having eaten all day and from the sudden dizzying fact of his triumph. "I'm still living . . . I'm walking out of here," he said.

Upstairs the Novaks' door was closed. When Mrs. Novak opened it, Ronald smiled eagerly and said, "Here it is—I found all of it!"

She looked at the stack of papers he was holding.

"I found every single page of it," he said. Mrs. Novak was nodding, as if she too were pleased, and over her shoulder Ronald caught a glimpse of a living room—it almost blinded him, lights reflecting from white walls, the striking gold and green and rust-colored furniture—and a child sitting on the floor, looking out this way. For some reason he felt a sudden rush of confusion, of error. He didn't know if he was talking or if Mrs. Novak was talking, congratulating him, but suddenly the words did not make sense and he really couldn't concentrate on them.

"I—I—"

Mrs. Novak must have seen something in his face, some sudden coalescence he himself did not know about. She stepped toward him as if to touch him. And at that moment his voice broke and he began to sob. "It isn't fair. . . . It isn't fair, I. . . ." He heard her exclaim softly, heard her ask what was wrong; she put her hand on his arm and must have been leaning very close to him, because he felt a strange, quivering, almost painful warmth along the length of his body. "I'm so afraid," he said. Then he began to sob convulsively and he knew that something terrible had happened to him. Mrs. Novak was murmuring to him, words of comfort that were mixed in with the warm powdery odor of her body, but he did not dare remain so close to her, he knew he had to get out of here before it was too late. He grabbed his trench coat and his briefcase and backed away.

She called after him, she called his name. But he half-ran to the stairs, sobbing. He got back to his own apartment at ten minutes to six.

PILGRIMS' PROGRESS

Wanda Barnett *is completing her doctoral studies in English at the University of Michigan and is currently a lecturer at Hilberry University.*

Saul Bird, *who received his Ph.D. in English from New York University, has taught in New York, California, Illinois, Louisiana, North Dakota, and Ontario. He is currently an Assistant Professor at Hilberry University and gave a talk, "The Graves of Academe," at a recent conference of the Humanities Association in Edmonton.*

Susannah Aptheker Bird *holds advanced degrees in history and French from Columbia University. She was Florence Tane Visiting Professor at Brandeis and is currently "retired" from teaching in order to complete her study of contemporary American drama. She is the author of* The Politics of Proust's Vision.

Philip Bird *was born in 1959.*

Erasmus Hubben *received his Ph.D. in philosophy at the University of Toronto and has done post-graduate work at Oxford and Princeton. Before joining the Hilberry philosophy department as an associate Professor, Dr. Hubben taught at the University of New Brunswick, Western Ontario, and the University of Manitoba. His book of poems,* Abstract Curiosities, *was published by the Little Press in 1957.*

Morris Kaye, Jr. *teaches psychology at Hilberry University. He describes himself as a "marginal academic." He holds a Master's Degree from Simon Fraser University.*

Homer McCrea *recently transferred to Hilberry University from York.*

Doris Marsdell, *from Chatham, is a third-year philosophy major at Hilberry.*

David Rose *is completing his undergraduate major in English and psychology.*

Wanda Barnett, born in 1945, received her bachelor's degree at Manhattanville College of the Sacred Heart in 1965, as class valedictorian, accepted a fellowship from the University of Michigan for graduate studies in English in the fall of that year, and in the spring of 1969 accepted a temporary lectureship at Hilberry University, a school in southern Ontario with an enrollment of about five thousand students. On September 9, 1969, she met Saul Bird; someone appeared in the doorway of her office at the University, rapping his knuckles loudly against the door. Wanda had been carrying a heavy box of books which she set down at once.

"How do you do, my name is Saul Bird," he said. He shook hands briskly with her. His voice was wonderfully energetic; it filled the narrow room and bounced off the empty walls, surrounding her. Wanda introduced herself, still out of breath from carrying the books; she smiled shyly. She leaned forward attentively, listening to Saul Bird, trying to understand what he was saying. He talked theatrically, elegantly. His voice wound about her like fine ribbon. She found herself stooping slightly so that she was not so obviously taller than he.

"What are your values? your standards? Everything in you will be questioned, eroded here, every gesture of spontaneity—if you love teaching, if you love working with young people, you've certainly come to the wrong university. Are you a Canadian? Where are you from? Have you found an apartment?—I can help you find one if you haven't."

"I have to look for an apartment today—"

"The economy is maniacal here. Are you a Canadian?"

"No, I'm from New York."

"Oh. New York." His voice went flat. He took time to light a cigarette and Wanda stared at him, bewildered. He had blond hair that was bunched and kinky about his face, like a cap; his face had looked young at first—the eyebrows that rose and fell dramatically, the expressive little mouth, the nose that twitched slightly with enthusiasm—but really it was the face of a forty-year-old, with fine, straight lines on the forehead and around the mouth. His complexion was both dark and pale—darkish pale, an olive hue, difficult to describe. He had a hot, busy, charming face. "I'm from New York too. I don't actually approve—I want to state this clearly—of this university's persistant policy of hiring Americans to fill positions that could be filled by Canadians, though I myself am an American, but I hope not contaminated by that country's madness —I am going to form a committee, incidentally, to investigate the depth of the Americanization of this university—Do you have a Ph.D.?"

"I'm writing my dissertation now," Wanda said quickly.

"On what?"

"Bunyan."

"Eh," he said flatly. The set of his face was now negative. He did not approve. Wanda nervously wiped her hands on her skirt. With one foot Saul Bird turned a box of books around so that he could read their titles. "Of course, all this is dead. Dried crap."

She stared at him in dismay.

His eyes darted quickly about her office. His profile was stern, prompt, oddly morose; the lines deepened about the small mouth. "These books. This office. The desk you've innocently inherited— from Jerry Renling, whom you will never meet, since they fired him last spring for taking too much interest in his students. All this is dead, finished. Where is your telephone?"

He turned back abruptly to her as if impatient with her slowness.

3 4

She came awake and said, "Here, it's here, let me move all this. . . ." She tried to pick up another box of books but the box gave way and some books fell onto the floor. She was very embarrassed. She cleared a space so that Saul Bird could use the telephone. He sat on the edge of her desk and dialled a number.

Wanda waited awkwardly. Should she leave her office while he telephoned? But he seemed to take no notice of her. His blond hair seemed to vibrate with electricity. On the bony ridge of his nose his black-rimmed glasses were balanced as if by an act of fierce will. . . . Why was her heart pounding so absurdly? It was the abrasive charge of his voice—that demanding, investigative air— it put her in mind of men she had admired, public men she had known only at a distance, a meek particpant in a crowd. Saul Bird had a delicate frame, but there was something powerful in the set of his shoulders and the precise, impatient way he dialled the telephone.

"Any messages there?" he said, without introducing himself. "What? Who? When will he call back?" He paused for a moment. Wanda brushed her short hair back nervously from her face. Was he talking to his wife? Was he married? "We have four more signatures on the petition. Yes. I *told* you to forget about that. It's twelve-ten now; can you get down here at one and pick me up? Why not? There's someone here looking for an apartment—"

Wanda stared at him. At that moment Saul Bird turned and smiled—fond, friendly, an intimate smile—or was she imagining it? He looked like a child in his dark turtleneck sweater and brown trousers. He wore sandals; the grimy straps looked gnawed. Wanda, in her stockings and new shoes, in her shapeless dress of dark cotton, felt foolishly tall in his sight: *why* had she grown so tall?

When he hung up he said, "My wife is on her way. We'll find you an apartment."

Someone appeared in the doorway, leaning in. "Saul?"

He was a young man in a soiled trench coat.

"Come in, I've been waiting for you," Saul Bird said. He introduced Wanda to the young man. "Wanda, this is Morris Kaye in psychology, my friend 'K.' This is Wanda Barnett. Susannah and I are going to find her an apartment this afternoon."

"Something has come up—Can I talk to you?"

"Talk."

"But it's about—I mean—" The young man glanced nervously at Wanda. He was about twenty-three, very tall, wearing a white T-shirt and shorts under his trench coat. His knees were pale beneath tufts of black hair. His face, dotted with small blemishes that were like cracked veins, had a strange glow, an almost luminous pallor. Wanda could feel his nervousness and shied away from meeting his eyes.

"We may as well introduce Wanda to the high style of this place," Saul Bird said. "I was given notice of non-renewal for next year. Which is to say, I have been fired. Why do you look so surprised?"

Wanda had not known she looked surprised—but now her face twitched as if eager to show these men that she was surprised, yes. "But what? Why?"

"Because they're terrified of me," Saul Bird said with a cold smile.

Susannah Aptheker Bird, born in 1928, earned doctoral degrees in both history and French from Columbia University. In the fall of 1958 she met and married Saul Bird. Their child, Philip, and Susannah's formidable book on Proust both appeared in 1959. The next year, Susannah taught at Brandeis while Saul Bird taught at a small experimental college in California; the following year they moved to Baton Rouge, where Susannah worked on her second book. When Saul Bird was dismissed from Louisiana State University, Susannah accepted an appointment at Smith College. The following year, however, she received a Frazer Foundation Grant to complete her second book—*The Radical Politics of Absurd Theater*—and decided to take a year's leave from teaching. Saul Bird had been offered a last-minute appointment from a small

Canadian university on the American border. The two of them
flew up to Hilberry University to look it over: they noted the ordinary, soot-specked buildings, the torn-up campus, the two or three
"modern" buildings under construction, the amiable, innocuous
student faces. They noted the grayness of the sky, which was the
same sky that arched over Niagara Falls, and which was fragrant
with gaseous odors and ominous as if the particles of soot were
somehow charged with energy, with electricity; not speaking, not
needing to speak, the Birds felt a certain promise in the very dis-
malness of the setting, as if it were not yet in existence, hardly yet
imagined.

They could bring it into existence.

On September 9, after Saul Bird called, Susannah changed her
clothes, taking off her pajama bottoms and putting on a pair of blue
jeans. The pajama top looked like a shirt—it was striped green and
white—and so she did not bother to change it. "Get dressed, your
father wants us to pick him up at the University," she said to the
boy, Philip. "I'm not leaving you here alone."

"Why not?" the boy said cheerfully. "You think I'd kill myself
or something?"

"To spite your father and me, you would."

The boy snickered.

She drove across town to the university to pick up Saul. He was
standing with a small group—"K" and a few students, Doris and
David and Homer, and a young woman whom Susannah did not
recognize. Saul introduced them: "This is Wanda Barnett, who is
anxious to get an apartment," Saul said as everyone piled into the
car. Wanda, demure and homely, seemed not to know what to do
with her hands. She squeezed in next to Susannah herself. She
smiled shyly, Susannah did not smile at all.

That was at one o'clock. By five that afternoon they had located
an apartment for Wanda, not exactly what she had wanted—she
had wanted to live within walking distance of the University—but
a fairly good apartment just the same, though quite expensive.
"Someone will have to wash these walls," Saul Bird declared to
the manager. "You don't expect this young woman to sign a lease

for such filth, do you? This city is still in the nineteenth century! Doris," he said to one of the students, "will you telephone Hubben for me? Tell him I'll be a little late. Well, Wanda, are you pleased with this?"

He turned to face her. She was exhausted, her stomach upset from the day's activity. Anxious not to disappoint Saul Bird she could only nod mutely. She felt how the others in the room—everyone except the child had come up—were waiting for her reaction, watching her keenly.

"Yes," she said shakily, "yes, it's perfect."

Saul Bird smiled.

"I'm on my way to a private conference with Hubben, I must leave, but we want you to have dinner with us tonight. I might be stopping at T. W.'s apartment to see what they've heard. Wanda, you're not busy tonight?"

"I really can't—"

"Why not?" Saul Bird frowned. He put out his arms and a cigarette burned eloquently in his fingers. Wanda felt the others watching her, waiting. Susannah Bird stood with her arms folded over the striped, sporty shirt she wore.

"I have work to do of my own, and I can't intrude upon you," Wanda said miserably.

"Relax. You take yourself too seriously," Saul Bird said. "You must re-assess yourself. You may be on the verge of a new life. You are in Canada, a country not free of bourgeois prostitution but relatively innocent, free at any rate of a foreign policy, a country that is a *possibility*. You will grant me that, that Canada is a possibility?"

Wanda glanced at the others. Saul Bird's wife had a thin, ravaged, shrewd face; it was set like stone, with patches of black hair like moss about it. A blank. "K" was staring at Wanda's shoes as if waiting painfully for her response. The students—Homer McCrea and David Rose—eyed her suspiciously. Their young nostrils widened with the rapidity of their breathing. Clearly, they did not trust her. Both were very thin. Their faces eagle-like and intense; in imitation of Saul Bird, perhaps, they wore turtleneck sweaters

38

that emphasized their thinness, and blue jeans and sandals. Their feet were grimy. Their toes were in perpetual movement, wiggling, as if the tension of the moment were unbearable. David Rose wore a floppy orange felt hat that was pulled down upon his head; his untidy hair stuck out around it. Homer McCrea, hatless, had a head of black curly hair and wore several rings on his fingers.

Wanda thought: *I must get away from these people.*

But Saul Bird said swiftly, as if he had heard her thoughts, "Why are you so nervous, Wanda? You look very tired. You look a little sick. Your problem is obvious to me—you do not relax. Always your mind is working and always you're thinking, planning, you're on guard, you're about to put up your hands to shield your private parts from us—why must you be so private? Why are you so terrified?"

"I—I don't know what you—"

"Come, we must leave. Susannah will make us all stuffed breast of veal."

A wave of nausea rose in Wanda. But she could not protest.

Erasmus Hubben, born in Toronto in 1930, completed his doctoral work in 1955 with an eight-hundred-page study called "The Classical Epistemological Relativism of Ernst Cassirer." Every summer Hubben travelled in Europe and Northern Africa; friends back in Canada received postcards scribbled over with his fine, enigmatic prose—sprinkled with exclamation points and generally self-critical, as if Hubben were embarrassed of himself. He was conscious of himself, always: students could not quite understand his nervous jokes, the facial tics and twitches that were meant to undercut the gravity of his pronouncements, the kind of baggy shuffling dance he did when lecturing. His face, seen in repose, was rather sorrowful, the eyebrows scanty so that the hard bone of his brow showed, the nose long and pale as wax, the lips thin and colorless; in company, his face seemed to flesh out, to become muscular with the drama of conversation, the pupils of the eyes blackening, the lips moving rapidly, so that tiny flecks of saliva gathered in the corners of his mouth. He was a good, generous man, and the somewhat clownish look of his clothes (seedy, baggy trousers with fallen seats; coats with elbows worn thin; shoes splotched with old mud) was half-deliberate, perhaps—while Hubben suggested to his colleagues, evasively and shyly, that they must play Monopoly with him sometime (he had invented a more complicated game of Monopoly) at the same time he waved away their pity for his loneliness by the jokes, the puns, the difficult allusions, the jolly cast of his face and dress alike . . . and he carried in his wallet the snapshot of a smiling, beefy young woman, which he took out often to show people as if to assure them that he had someone, yes, there was someone back in Toronto, someone existed somewhere who cared for Erasmus Hubben.

He came to Hilberry University in 1967, having resigned his position at another university for reasons of health. He taught logic, but his real love was poetry, and he had arranged for a private printing of a book of his poems. They were always short, often ending with queries—

Actual adversaries
are not as prominent as quivering
speculations

When you think of me, my dear,
do you think of
anything?

He took teaching very seriously. He liked students, though he did not understand them; he liked their energy, their youth, their *foreignness*. During his first year at Hilberry he prepared for as many as twenty hours for a single lecture. But his teaching was not successful. He could not understand why. So he worked harder on his lectures, taking notes by hand so that he would not disturb the family he lived with. (He boarded with a colleague and his family.) Late in the winter of 1969 a student named David Rose came to see him. This student did not attend class very often, and he was receiving a failing grade, but when he sat in class with his arms folded, his face taut and contemptuous beneath a floppy orange felt hat, he impressed Hubben as a superior young man. Wasn't that probably a sign of superiority, his contempt? Erasmus Hubben shook hands with him, delighted that a student would seek him out, and made a joke about not seeing him very often. David Rose smiled slowly, as if not getting the joke. He was very thin and intense. "Dr. Hubben," he said, "I have been designated to approach you with this question—would you like your class liberated?" Hubben was leaning forward with an attentive smile—*liberated*? "Yes. Your course is obviously a failure. Your subject is not entirely hopeless, but you are unable to make it relevant. Your teaching methods are dead, dried up, finished. Of course, as a human being, you have potential," the boy said. Hubben blinked. He could not believe what he was hearing. The boy went on to explain that a certain professor in English, Saul Bird, was conducting experimental classes and that the other Hilberry professors would do well to learn from him before it was too late. Saul— everyone called him "Saul"—did not teach classes formally at all; he had "liberated" his students; he met with them at his apartment or in the coffee shop or elsewhere, usually at night, his students read and did anything they wanted, and those who skipped all sessions were free to do so since in any case they were going to be allowed to grade themselves at the end of the year. "The old-fashioned grading system," David Rose said angrily, "is nothing but a form of imperialistic sadism! Don't you think so?"

Hubben stared at the boy. He had been hearing about Saul Bird for a long time, and he had seen the man at a distance—hurrying across campus, usually dressed badly, with a few students running along with him—but he had never spoken to him. Something about Saul Bird's intense, urbane, theatrical manner had frightened Hubben off. And then there was the matter of his being a Jew, his being from New York . . . Hubben's family was a little prejudiced, and though Hubben himself was free of such nonsense he did not exactly seek out people like Saul Bird. So he told David Rose, with

41

a gracious smile, that he would be delighted to talk with "Saul" sometime. He hoped he wasn't too old to learn how to teach! David Rose did not catch this joke, but gravely and politely nodded. "Yes, the whole university better learn. It better learn from Saul or go under," he said.

Soon, he began to hear of little else except Saul Bird. Bird had been fired and would fulfill only the next year's contract. His department—English—and the Dean of Arts and Sciences had voted to dismiss him. Now it seemed that many of Hubben's students were also "Saul's" students. They sat together in the classroom, when they came to class, their arms folded, their eyes beady and undefeated though Hubben's finely-wrought lectures obviously bored them. David Rose had enrolled for another course, still wearing his orange hat; a girl named Doris had joined him, perhaps his girl friend—Doris all angles and jutting lines, very thin, with stringy blond hair and sweaters pulled down to her bony hips as if they were men's sweaters, her voice sometimes rising in a sarcastic whine that startled the other students, "Professor Hubben, doesn't this entirely contra*dict* what you said the other day?" Another boy, Homer McCrea, had black curly hair and a dramatic manner that put Hubben in mind of Saul Bird. Sometimes he took notes all period long (were these lectures notes going to be used against him?—Hubben wondered), sometimes he sat with his arms folded, his expression distant and critical. Hubben began to talk faster and faster, he spiced up his lectures with ironic little jokes of the sort that superior students would appreciate, but nothing worked— nothing worked.

Saul Bird came to see him the first week in September, striding into his office. "I'm Saul Bird. I would like your signature on a petition," he said. Hubben spent many minutes reading the petition, examining its syntax, to give himself time to think. Saul Bird's presence in this small room upset him. The man was very close, physically close to Hubben—and Hubben could not stand to be touched—and he was very *real*. He kept leaning over Hubben's shoulder to point out things in the petition. "*That* is the central issue. *That* will break someone's back," Saul Bird said. Hubben, rattled, could not make much sense of the petition except that it seemed to support excellence in teaching and the need for dedication to students and for experimentation to prevent "the death of the humanities." Hubben could not see that it had much to do with the case of Saul Bird at all. But he said, not meeting Saul Bird's stare, "I really must decline. I'm afraid I don't sign things."

"You what?"

"I'm afraid I don't. . . ."

"You refuse to involve yourself?" Saul Bird said sharply.

Hubben sat staring at the petition. He read it over again. Would this awful man not go away?

"I think you'll reconsider if you study my case," Saul Bird said. "Most of the faculty is going to support me, once the injustice of the case is aired. Here is my own file—read it tonight and tell me what your response is." And he gave Hubben a manila folder of Xeroxed memos, outlines, programs, personal letters from students in praise of Saul Bird, dating back to March of the year that Saul Bird had signed a contract with Hilberry. Hubben sat dizzily looking through these things. He had his own work to do. . . . What sense could he make of all this?

On September 9 he was to meet with Saul Bird at four in the afternoon, but the hour came and went. He was immensely relieved. He prepared to go home, thinking of how much better it was to stay away from people, really. No close relationships. No intimate ties. Of course, he liked to "chat" with people—particularly about intellectual subjects—and he enjoyed the simple-minded family dinners in the Kramer household, where he boarded. He liked students at a distance. Women made him extremely nervous. His female students were colorful as partridges and as unpredictable—so many sudden flutterings, the darting of eyes and hands! The young men in his classes were fine human beings but, up close, the heat of their breath was disturbing. Better to keep people as a distance. . . . And as Hubben thought this clearly to himself, the telephone rang and Doris Marsdell announced that Saul Bird was on his way. "But he's an hour late and I'm going home," Hubben protested. "You hadn't better go home," the girl said. "What?" said Hubben. "What did you say, Miss Marsdell?" "This is a matter of extreme importance, more to you than to Saul. You *hadn't better go home.*" Shaken, Hubben looked around his dingy, cluttered office as if seeking help —but he was alone. The girl went on quickly, "Saul is a genius, a saint. You people all know that! You're jealous of him! You want to destroy him because you're jealous, you're terrified of a real genius in your midst!" "Miss Marsdell," Hubben said, "are you joking? You must be joking." "I don't joke," the girl said, and hung up.

When Saul Bird arrived fifteen minutes later he was in an excellent mood. He shook hands briskly, lit a cigarette, and sat on the edge of Hubben's desk. "Did you read my file? Are you convinced of the injustice of this university?"

Hubben was extremely warm. "I'm not sure—"

"Most of your colleagues in Philosophy are going to sign in my behalf," Saul Bird said. "What is your decision?"

"I wasn't aware that most of them were—"

"Of course not. People are afraid to talk openly of these matters."

"I still don't think—"

"My wife wants you to have dinner with us tonight. We'll talk about this quietly, sanely. Intelligent discourse between humanists is the only means of bringing about a revolution—until the need for violence is more obvious, I mean," Saul Bird said with a smile.

"Violence?" Hubben stared. He felt something in his blood warming, opening, coming to life as if in arrogant protestation against himself, his own demands. He was very warm. Saul Bird, perched on the edge of his desk, eyed him through glasses that looked as if they might slightly magnify the images that came through them.

"People like you," Saul Bird said softly, "have been allowed to live through books for too long. That's been your salvation—dust and the droppings of tradition—but all that is ending, as you know. You'll change. You'll be changed. My wife would like you to come to dinner. You're rooming with the Kramers, aren't you? Old Harold Kramer and his 'ethics of Christianity' seminar?"

Hubben wanted to protest that Kramer was only forty-six.

"People like Kramer, according to the students, are hopeless. They must go under. People like *you*—and a very few others—are possibilities. The students do admit certain possibilities. They are very wise, these twenty-year-olds, extraordinarily wise. The future belongs to them, of course. You are not anti-student, are you?"

"Of course not, but—"

"Telephone Kramer's wife and tell her you're eating out tonight," Saul Bird said.

Hubben hesitated. Then something in him surrendered: really, it would not harm him to have dinner with the Birds. He was curious about them, after all. And then it could not be denied that Saul Bird was a fascinating man. His face was shrewd, peaked, oddly appealing. He was obviously very intelligent—his students had not exaggerated. Hubben had heard, of course, that Saul Bird had been fired for incompetence and "gross misconduct." He did not teach his classes, evidently. He did not assign any examinations or papers and his students were allowed to "grade" themselves. But in the man's presence these charges faded, they did not seem quite *relevant*. . . . Hubben made up his mind. He would spend the evening with the Birds. Wasn't it a part of the rich recklessness of life, to explore all possibilities?

And so it all began.

The group met informally at Saul Bird's apartment, at first two or three times a week, then every evening. Wanda came as often as she could—she had to work hard on her class preparations and on her dissertation, she was often exhausted, a little sick to her stomach, and doubtful of her subject (*Eh*, Saul Bird had said flatly)—but still she showed up, shy and clumsy about this new part of her life. Saul Bird and his group were so passionate! They were so wise! They asked her bluntly how she could devote her intelligence to the analysis of an insane 17th-century preacher when the world

45

about her was so rotten? It was based upon hypocrisy and exploitation, couldn't she see? The world was a nightmarish joke, unfunny. Nothing was funny. It was a fact of this life, Saul Bird lectured to his circle, that *nothing was funny*.

And he would stare openly at Erasmus Hubben, whose nervous jokes had annoyed the circle at first.

Hubben was transformed gradually. How had he been blind for so long? His students told him that half the faculty was going to be fired, hounded out, shamed out of existence, if Saul Bird was not rehired. When Saul Bird was rehired, however, he would not be gratefully silent but would head a committee of activist faculty and students to expose the hypocrisy of the rest of the faculty. Their findings would be published. Would he, Erasmus, like to contribute anything to help with printing costs? As the fall semester went on Hubben turned up at Saul Bird's more and more often, he stayed later, he became quite dependent upon these nightly meetings. How was it possible that he had known so little about himself? about his own stultifying life? He began to speak wildly, as if parodying his own professorial manner, and the saliva flew from his lips. He believed that Saul Bird listened closely to him. The very air of Saul Bird's crowded little apartment was exhilarating to Hubben; he and two other faculty members who showed up regularly began to feel younger, to dress in an untidy, zestful, youthful manner. Hubben gained a new respect for Morris Kaye, whom he had never taken seriously. And a new lecturer, a young woman named Wanda, attracted Hubben's eye: vague in her speech, flat-chested, her eyes watery with emotion or shyness, she did not upset Hubben at all and she seemed to admire his speeches.

On the walls of the apartment there were many posters and photographs, and those that caught Hubben's eye often were of blazing human beings—Buddhist monks and nuns, and a Czechoslovakian university student. A human being in flames! Maniacal flames leaping up from an oddly rigid, erect human being, sitting cross-legged in a street! It was unimaginable. But it had happened, it had been photographed. Hubben had the idea as the weeks passed that only so dramatic an act, so irreparable an act, would impress Saul Bird.

46

When Wanda could not come to the apartment she thought about the group and could not concentrate on her work. What were they talking about? They usually talked for hours—sometimes quietly, sometimes noisily. The air would be heavy with smoke. Everyone except Wanda smoked, even Saul Bird's little boy showed up, smoking. (The Birds did not exactly live together. Susannah had an apartment on the top floor of a building, and Saul had a smaller apartment on the second floor, in the rear.) The little boy, Phillip, would come down to visit and stand behind his father's chair, watching everyone. He was a fascinating child, Wanda thought. She feared children, usually, but Philip did not seem to be a child; he was dwarfish rather than small, wise and almost wooden, with thick kinky hair a little darker than his father's, and his father's cool, intelligent face. He would not attend public schools, and the Birds supported him. (A legal case was going on over this.) He said little, unlike other children Wanda had known, and she was very pleased one day when the Birds asked her to take Philip out to get a pair of shoes. She took him on the bus. He was silent except for one remark: "Don't fall in love with my father, please."

Wanda laughed hysterically.

She began to lie awake at night, thinking about Saul Bird. He often looked directly at her, pointedly at her. He often nodded in support of her remarks. If only they could talk alone! —but the apartment was always crowded with students who were staying overnight, some of them with sleeping bags. The young man with the orange hat, David Rose, had moved out of his parents' house and Saul Bird had gladly agreed to house him, for nothing. The telephone was always ringing. Susannah sometimes showed up around midnight, silent and dark. She reminded Wanda of a crow. But the woman was brilliant, her book on Proust was brilliant! Wanda despaired of such brilliance, herself. Susannah had a deft, witch-like, whimsical style, her small face sometimes breaking into a darting, razorish smile that was really charming. And her wit frightened everyone—"If my husband could function normally, he would function normally," she said once, winking. And Hubben was always there. He sent out for pizzas and chop suey and hamburgers. "K"—"I am a character out of Kafka, pure essence," he declared—was always there. And the students, always the students. They seemed to live on air, disdaining Hubben's offers of food. They did not need food. They lived on the hours of intense, intoxicating dialogue—

Saul Bird: What conclusions have you come to?

Doris: That I was an infant. I was enslaved.

Saul Bird: And what now?

Doris: Now I am totally free.

Saul Bird: You're exaggerating to gain our respect.

Doris: No, I'm free. I'm free. I detest my parents and everything they stand for—I'm free of them—I am my own woman, entirely!

During the day, Hubben began to notice that his colleagues at the university were jealous of him. They were probably curious about the renewed interest in his notoriously difficult subject, logic. How strange, that young people should begin to hang around Erasmus Hubben's office! Hubben spent hours "chatting" with them. *I must get closer. I must wake up to reality*, he thought. His colleagues were not only jealous of his popularity, but fearful of it. He began closing his office door and opening it only to Saul Bird's circle. He took around Saul Bird's petition and tried to argue people into signing it. When Kramer would not sign it, Hubben became extremely angry and moved out of the Kramer home and into a cheap riverfront hotel. He told the Kramers that their attitude toward Saul Bird was disgusting. They were sick people, he could not live under the same roof with such sick, selfish people! Kramer, a professor of ethics, an old-fashioned Catholic layman, was brought to tears by Hubben's accusations. But Hubben would not move back. He would not compromise with his new ideals.

"I have friends now. I have real friends," he thought fifty times a day, in amazement. He doodled out little poems, smiling at their cryptic ingenuity—

> One savage kiss is worth
> a thousand savage syllogisms—

and showed them to Saul Bird, who shrugged his shoulders. Though he was a professor of English, Saul had not much interest in poetry. He argued that the meaning of life was *action*, involvement with other *human* beings, the trappings of the past were finished—books, lectures, classrooms, buildings, academic status! He, Saul Bird, was being fired only because he represented the future. The Establishment feared the future. In a proclamation sent to the local newspaper, calling for an investigation of the financial holdings of the university's Board of Governors, he stated: "Because it is my duty to liberate the students of this university I am being fired. Because people like myself—and we are numerous in Canada and the United States—are loyal to our students and not to the Establishment, we are being persecuted. But we are going to fight back."

"We certainly are going to fight back!" Hubben cried.

He hurried about the university with a wild, happy look. He felt so much younger! Though living in the White Hawk Hotel did not agree with him, he felt much younger these days; it was mysterious. He and the young lecturer, Wanda Barnett, often sought each other out at the university to discuss the change in their lives. At first they were shy; then, guessing at their common experiences, they began to talk quite openly. "I was always lonely. I was always left out. I was always the tallest girl in my class," Wanda said, gulping for breath. Hubben, feeling a kind of confused, sparkling gratitude for this woman's honesty, admitted that he, too, had been lonely, isolated, overly-intelligent, a kind of freak. "And I was selfish, so selfish! I inherited from my father—a pious old fraud!—an absolute indifference to moral and political commitment. I skipped a stage in the natural evolution of mankind! But thanks to Saul—"

"Yes, thanks to Saul—" Wanda said at once.

Just before the break at Christmas, the University's Appeals Committee turned down the Saul Bird case.

"And now we must get serious," Saul Bird said to the circle.

They began to talk of tactics. They talked of faculty resignations, of the denunciation of the university by its student population; guardedly, at first, they talked of demonstrations and breakage and bombings. They would certainly occupy the Humanities Building and only violent police action could get them out—maybe not even

49

that, if they were armed. They could stay in the building for weeks and force the university's administration to re-hire Saul Bird. As they spoke they became more excited, more certain of themselves. The blazing suicides on Saul Bird's walls were luminous as if in sympathy with their cause.

How could one live in such a rotten society? Why not destroy it with violence?

The telephone was always ringing. Sometimes Wanda answered, sometimes one of the girl students; if Saul Bird nodded, they handed the receiver over to him, if he shook his head they made excuses for him. He was not always available to everyone. This pleased them immensely, his belonging to *them*. When they did not talk directly of forcing the administration to re-hire him, they talked about him, about his effect on their lives. They were frank and solemn. A first-year Arts student, a girl, clasped her hands before her and said breathlessly, "Saul has changed me. No cell in me is the same." "K," enormously moved, sat on the floor and confessed, "He revolutionized my concept of reality. It's like that corny Gestalt of George Washington's face—once it's pointed out to you, you can't see anything else. Not lines and squiggles, but only Washington's face. That is fate."

But sometimes, very late at night, the discussions became more intimate. It was in January that Saul Bird turned to Hubben, who had been unusually noisy that evening, and said, "You assure us you've been transformed. But I doubt it. I doubt that you are ready yet to face the truth about yourself."

"The truth?"

"The truth. Will you tell us?"

It was so late at night—around four o'clock—that only about twelve students remained, as well as Wanda, "K," and a recent convert, a peppy, bearded sociology lecturer. The air was suddenly quite tense. Everyone looked at Hubben, who tugged at the collar of his rumpled shirt.

"I don't know what you mean, Saul," he said.

"Of course you know what I mean."

"That I'm prejudiced? Against certain races . . . or creeds . . .?"

Saul Bird was silent.

"I admit to a slight primitive fear . . . an entirely irrational fear of people different from myself. It's Toronto instinct! Good old Anglo-Saxon stock," Hubben laughed.

"We know all that," David Rose said coldly.

"How do you know that? Did you—did you know that?" Hubben said. He looked around the room. Wanda Barnett was watching him, her face drawn with the late hour. "K" 's look was slightly glazed. "But I like all human beings personally, as—as human beings—Today I was chatting in the lounge with Franklin Ambrose, and it never occurred to me, not once, that he was a—that he was a Negro—"

Hubben looked miserably at Saul Bird.

"Franklin Ambrose is not a Negro," said Saul Bird shrewdly.

Everyone barked with laughter. It was true: Frank Ambrose, a black man of thirty whose Ph.D. was from Harvard, who dressed expensively and whose clipped high style was much appreciated by his female students, was not really a "Negro" at all.

"What about Jews, Erasmus?" Doris Marsdell said suddenly.

"Jews? I don't think about Jews. I have no feelings one way or another. I do not think about people as Jews—or non-Jews—"

"Tell us more," another student said with a snicker.

"Yes, tell us."

"Tell us about your most intimate instinct," Saul Bird said. He leaned forward to stare down at Hubben, who was sitting on the floor. "What is the truth about your feeling for me?"

"Extreme admiration—"

"Come, come. I think we all know. You might as well admit it."

"Admit what?"

"Your inclinations."

"But what—what are my inclinations?"

"Your obsession."

Huben stared. "What do you mean?"

"Tell us."

"But what—what do you mean?"

"Your desire for me," Saul Bird said.

"I don't—"

51

"Your homosexual desire for me," Saul Bird said flatly.

Hubben sat without moving.

"Well?" said Saul Bird. "Why are you so silent?"

"I don't—I don't—" Hubben wiped his forehead with both hands. He could not bear the gaze of Saul Bird but there was nowhere else to look. And then, suddenly, he heard his own voice saying, "Yes, I admit it. It's true."

Saul Bird lifted his hands in a gesture that mached the lifting of his eyebrows. "Of course it's true," he said.

The discussion leapt at once to another topic: tactics for the occupation of the Humanities Building. Hubben took part vociferously in this discussion. He stayed very late, until only he and a few students remained, and Saul Bird said curtly, "I forgot to tell you that Susannah and I are flying to New York this morning. Will you all go home so that I can get some sleep?"

"You're going away?" everyone said.

A weekend without Saul Bird was a lonely weekend. Hubben did not leave the White Hawk Hotel; Wanda, staying up in Susannah's apartment in order to take care of Philip, hoped for a telephone call. While the child read books on mathematical puzzles, or stared for long periods of time out the window, Wanda tried to prepare her Chaucer lectures. But she could not concentrate: she kept thinking of Saul Bird.

Who could resist Saul Bird?

The White Hawk Hotel was very noisy and its odors were of festivity and rot. Hubben, unable to sleep, telephoned members of the Saul Bird circle during the night, chatting and joking with them, his words tumbling out, saliva forming in the corners of his mouth. Sometimes he himself did not know what he was saying. After talking an hour and a half with "K" about the proper wording of their letters of resignation, he caught himself up short and asked, startled, "Why did you call me? Has anything happened?"

The next Monday on his way to class, he overheard two students laughing behind him. He whirled around; the boys stared at him, their faces hardening. No students of his. He did not know them.

But perhaps they knew him?

5 2

down his trousers and step out of them! And then, eluding everyone, he ran along the side of the building, through the bushes, in his underclothes.

"Get him, get him!" people cried. A few students tried to head him off, but he turned suddenly and charged right into them. He was screaming. Wanda, confused, stood on the steps and could not think what to do—then two young girls ran right into her, uttering high, shrill, giggling little screams. They were from her 17th-century class. They ran right into her and she slipped on the icy steps and fell. She could not get up. Someone's foot crashed onto her hand. About her head were feet and knees; everyone was shouting. Someone stumbled backward and fell onto Wanda, knocking her face down against the step, and she felt a violent pain in her mouth.

She began to weep helplessly.

Saul Bird, who had thought it best to stay away from the occupation, telephoned Wanda at three o'clock in the morning. He spoke rapidly and angrily. "Come over here at once, please. Susannah and I are driving to Chicago in an hour and we need you to sit with Philip. I know all about what happened—spare me the details, please."

"But poor Erasmus—"

"How soon can you get here?"

"Right away," Wanda said. Her mouth was swollen—one of her teeth was loose and would probably have to be pulled. But she got dressed and called a taxi and ran up the steps into Saul Bird's apartment building. In the foyer a few students were waiting. Doris Marsdell cried, "What are you doing? Is he letting you come up to see him?" Her eyes were pink and her voice hysterical. "Did anything happen? Is he still alive? He didn't attempt suicide, did he?"

"He asked me to take care of Philip for a few days," Wanda said.

"*You*? He asked *you*?" Doris cried in dismay.

Susannah answered the door. She was wearing a yellow tweed

pants suit and hoop earrings; her mouth was a dark, heavy pink. "Come in, come in!" she said cheerfully. The telephone was ringing. Saul Bird, knotting a necktie, appeared on the run. "Don't answer that telephone!" he said to Susannah. The boy, Philip, stood in his pajamas at a window, his back to the room. Everywhere there were suitcases and clothes. Wanda tried to cover her swollen mouth with her hand, ashamed of looking so ugly. But Saul Bird did not look at her. He was rummaging through some clothes. "Wanda, we'll contact you in a few days. We're on our way out of this hellhole," he said curtly.

She helped them carry their suitcases down to the car.

Then, for two days, she stayed in the apartment and "watched" Philip. She fingered her loose tooth, which was very painful; she wept, knotting a handkerchief in her fingers. She could not shake loose her cold. "Do you think—do you think your father will ever recover from this?" she asked, staring at the little boy.

He spent most of his time reading and doodling mathematical puzzles. When he laughed it was without humor, a short breathy bark.

Saul Bird did not telephone until the following Saturday, and then he had little to say. "Put Philip on the Chicago flight at noon. Give him the keys to both apartments."

"But aren't you coming back?"

"Never," said Saul Bird.

"But what about your teaching?—your students?" Wanda cried.

"I've had it at Hilberry University," Saul Bird said.

She was paralyzed.

Preparing Philip for the trip, she walked about in a kind of daze. She kept saying, "But your father must return. He must fight them. He must insist upon justice." Philip did not pay much attention to her. A cigarette in the center of his pursed lips, he combed his thick hair carefully, preening in the mirror. He was a squat, stocky, and yet attractive child—like his father, his face wooden and theatrical at once, a sickly olive hue. Wanda stared at him. He was all she had now, her last link with Saul Bird. "Do you think he's desperate? Will he be hospitalized like poor Erasmus Hubben? What will happen?"

"Nothing," said Philip.

"What do you mean?"

"He has found another job, probably."

"What? How do you know?" Wanda cried.

"This has happened before," said Philip.

In the taxi to the airport she began to weep desperately. She kept touching the child's hands, his arms. "But what will happen to us . . . to me . . .? The year is almost gone, I have nothing to show for it, I resigned from the University and I cannot, I absolutely cannot ask to be rehired like the others . . . I cannot degrade myself! And my dissertation, all that is dead, dried up, all that belongs to the past! What will happen to me? Will your father never come back, will I never see him again?"

"My father," said Philip coldly, "has no particular interest in women."

Wanda hiccuped with laughter. "I didn't mean—"

"He makes no secret of it. I've heard him talk about it dozens of times," Philip said. "He was present at my birth. Both he and my mother wanted this. He watched me born . . . me being born . . . he watched all that blood, my mother's insides coming out . . . all that blood. . . ." The child was dreamy now, no longer abrasive and haughty; he stared past Wanda's face as if he were staring into a mystery. His voice took on a softened, almost bell-like tone. "Oh, my father is very articulate about that experience. . . . Seeing that mess, he said, made him impotent forever. Ask him. He'd love to tell you about it."

"I don't believe it," Wanda whispered.

"Then don't believe it."

She waited until his flight was called and walked with him to the gate. She kept touching his hands, his arms, even his bushy dark-blond hair. He pulled away from her, scowling; then, as if taking pity on her, staring with sudden interest at her bluish, swollen lip, he reached out to shake hands. It was a formal handshake, a farewell.

"But what will I do with the rest of my life?" Wanda cried.

The child shook his head. "You are such an obvious woman," he said flatly.

UP FROM SLAVERY

A decade before the phrase "Black is Beautiful" became popular, Franklin Ambrose knew that he was beautiful. But his beauty had nothing to do with being black. He was naturally handsome in a small, neat way; he cultivated a thin moustache and a very black, rugged, almost savage goatee; his shoes were so shiny that they looked varnished; he wore Pierre Cardin shirts of various peacock-gay colors, expensive silk twill ties and ascots, and suits whose notched and peaked lapels expanded and narrowed according to fashion laws totally unknown to Frank's mundane, hard-working colleagues at the University. He took an obvious, healthy pride in physical appearances and was critical of his wife's clothes, which always seemed shapeless and dowdy. "Do you want to embarrass me?" he sometimes asked in exasperation.

But most of the time he was cheerful and very energetic. He hastened to put all white people at their ease, immediately, by emphasizing the scorn he felt for anything "black" (he hated that modish word; he preferred the more sanitary and middle-class "Negro"). In fact, he accepted a position at a small university in Southern Canada, near Hamilton, because he suspected—correctly—that there would be few Negroes in the school. He had only one real rival—a popular professor of psychology who sported an Afro hair-cut and love beads, but Franklin put him down by saying, whenever the man's name was mentioned: "There's a real professional black." This made his white friends laugh appreciatively.

Franklin was not "black," but he was very professional. His degrees were all from Harvard and he had spent a year in England as a Fulbright Fellow; during that time he had developed a faint, clipped English accent. At Harvard he had been very popular with Radcliffe girls, especially a kind of bright, intense Jewish girl who shared many of his interests in literature and music. But he wanted to marry another kind of girl—he didn't know why, exactly—he had his heart set on a Wellesley girl whose father was a judge in Boston, a sweet girl, not very intelligent but gifted with a pale, smooth, flawless complexion. Their marriage was violently opposed by her family but Franklin won, and in 1965 he accepted a position a Hilberry University and brought his bride to a small city in southwestern Ontario: with great anticipation, a sense of drama, for he was the only Negro in the English Department and the only Harvard man.

Frank became the Department's most popular professor immediately. And yet something began to go wrong in the second year: he felt a strange, aimless melancholy, his classroom successes were coming too easily, he noticed that he and Eunice, out together, no longer attracted the attention and the occasional outraged glares they had attracted in the past. No doubt about it, Eunice was becoming dowdy, her waist and hips thickening; she was not even very pretty, when you looked closely. The only happiness in Frank's life were his twin sons, wonderfully light, almost fair-skinned little boys, with beautiful features—especially their eyes. Sometimes Frank stared at them, unable to quite believe the miracle of their physical beauty. How had anything so wonderful happened to *him?*

But he tended to forget about them; as his wife's looks dwindled and he began to sink into the ordinary routine of teaching in an ordinary university—no over-wrought, neurotic, brilliant Radcliffe girls to stimulate his appetite!—he felt at times a sense of panic, of loss. He was twenty-eight years old, a shock. Then he was thirty. His sense of loss was almost physical, as if he were actually hungry for something, without knowing what it was. For his thirty-second birthday he gifted himself with a white MG, though his wife and sons obviously could not crowd into it with him. He bought an elegant, costly smoking jacket to wear in his study at home, and a suede calfskin belted coat that drew all eyes to it as he strolled across campus. He began going with students to The Cave, a popular pub, crowded and noisy and darkly merry. Most of his student-friends were boys, who were surprised and pleased that a professor of Frank's stature should bother with them—the other professors nervously avoided all personal contact with students—but a few were girls. They were all the same type, more or less: intellectual, casual, a litle brazen, a litle sloppy, and they seemed to appreciate Frank even more than the boys did.

A possibility dawned on Frank.

Yes, he was attracted to the girls as if to searing, caressing rays of light: their pale skins, their moving, twisting, smirking, giggling mouths, their tight, thigh-high skirts, their nervous writhing mannerisms when they came in for "conferences" to his office. They brushed their long hair out of their eyes and smiled at him. Frank would feel at such times an intoxication that forced him to lean forward, gazing at them, his own eyes bright and his flesh livened by their closeness. They complained to him about their families, or their other professors, or their boy friends: "My boy friend is, I don't know, he's so *dumb* compared to someone like you, Dr. Ambrose. . . . I mean, he's so *dumb* when it comes to conversation that I just sort of blank out and think about, well, you, I guess, I mean I think about how funny you were in class or something and . . . well . . . I think about *you* when I'm with him, you know, when the two of us are . . . you know . . . I feel real rotten about it because it isn't fair I guess to him because we're really sort of in love . . . and . . . and. . . ." And they would gaze at Frank with their eyes sometimes misting over. At such times he felt his heart beat with certainty: *Unmistakable!*

The girls were so sweet, with their kisses and their sudden, rationed tears, that Frank went about in a perpetual daze, more genial than ever before.

Being a gentleman, he made no more than the most subtle allusions to his colleagues in the Department, most of whom were prematurely weary, slowed-down with families, balding, thickening, and yet still fired feebly with hopes of romance; they were temporarily freshened by stray rumors of secret liaisons, even though the liaisons never happened to them. They appreciated Frank, who was, after all, "black" (the word began to be used, cautiously, around 1969-70), so trim and handsome and elegantly turned out, and they quipped that he was their "liaison" man with the students.

"Frank will bridge the generation gap for us," they said with wistful, encouraging smiles.

But then, in the late Sixties, an essay with the title "The Student as Nigger" became widely circulated; it was even published in the student newspaper. Frank was aghast. He couldn't believe it. Colleagues and students began talking quite familiarly, openly, of the oppression of students and "niggers"—often in Frank's presence, as if to demonstrate to him how liberal and understanding they were. *The word "nigger"! On everyone's lips!* Frank was furious, demoralized, befuddled; he would not explain his moods to his wife; he went out one evening by himself to a cocktail lounge far from the University, where he got drunk and had to be sent home in a taxi-cab. At such times, when he was very drunk, he had the confused idea that some white man—any white man at all—was trying to appropriate his twin boys. "They want to take my babies away, my babies," he would weep. "They want to take my babies because I'm black and my babies are white . . . ."

He knew he was not a "nigger" and yet he wasn't sure that other people, glancing at him, knew. He recalled with horror the evening, at a faculty party, when the slightly drunken wife of a colleague had cornered him to ask whether he planned "to go back to the ghetto to help his people," seeing that he himself was so successful. That white bitch! How he had hated her!

But his young girl students fawned over him, even pursued him, singly and in small packs. There was no doubt of his manhood with *them.* Their names were Cindy and Laurie and Sandy and Cheryl, they passed in and out of his arms with the rotation of the academic semesters, some of them wise and cynical with experience, others incredibly naive and therefore dangerous, they were like

66

figures in the most riotous, improbable of his adolescent dreams, somehow lacking substance, lacking souls, because of their very eagerness to oblige him. "But Dr. Ambrose, you're a genius from Harvard and all that, I'm afraid to talk to you, I'm afraid you're giving me a grade when you just *look* at me!" One of the Cindys or Sandys whose bold stare had misled Frank nearly caused a scandal by confessing to her parents, who in turn called the University's President and several members of the Board of Trustees . . . but after a four-hour conference in the President's office Franklin managed to be forgiven. He promised not to be "indiscreet" again.

That was in the winter of 1969. In the spring of that year, the Appointments & Promotion Committee (called the "Hiring & Firing" Committee) of the Department interviewed applicants for the position of lecturer in English. Franklin was the youngest member of this powerful committee, and he grilled candidates for the job seriously. He was not very impressed with a young Ph.D. from Yale, nor with a young Indian student from Oxford; he was very impressed with a young woman named Molly Holt, who rushed in fifteen minutes late for her interview, wearing a very short leather skirt and bright gold boots. . . .

Franklin stared at this girl. She was no more than five foot one or two, and therefore shorter than he. She was very pretty, with a small, pixie-like face, blond hair snipped short and puffed out carelessly about her face, so young, so pretty, with impressive recommendations from the University of Chicago. . . . ! It was hard to believe. Frank's interest in her grew as he glanced through her application and saw that she was a divorcée with a three-year-old son. She was answering questions pertly and brightly. Obviously an intelligent woman. Frank was careful to ask her questions that might lead her to admirable statements: "I am deeply committed to literature and to teaching, yes," she said. "And to the future, to the struggle for equality between men and women. . . ." Hastily, Frank asked her about her doctoral thesis, which she had just begun: "It's called *Crises of Sexual Identity in Trollope and Dickens*," she said. "It grew out of my fascination with the role of women in Victorian literature. Imagine, Charles Dickens created Edith Dombey!—and yet in his personal life he was such a bastard, a real male chauvinist pig—"

After this, it took Frank several hours and several meetings of the Committee to hire Miss Holt: he had a lot of talking to do.

When she arrived in September he drove her around in his neat little white sportscar, helping her locate an apartment, helping her unpack books (she had a small mountain of books); he lent himself out as her escort at University functions for the first few weeks. Someone sent his wife an anonymous note that said *Your husband is extremely attentive to a certain young lady professor*, but Frank tore it up with such contempt and such finesse that his wife could not help believing him, though she wept. Frank, in Molly Holt's company, was careful to be polite and witty and distant, never staring too boldly at her or taking up her vivacious comments—she was always complimenting him on his clothes—as if he feared what might happen might happen too quickly. Molly herself dressed rather flamboyantly, for a young lady with her rigorous academic background (before Chicago she had gone to Bennington); she was always hurrying through the Department's corridors in mini-skirts and serapes and boots and then, as the fashions gradually changed, in pants-suits that clung tightly to her firm, intense little body. At Department meetings she was a little arch; she sometimes interrupted people, even the Head of the Department, a small white-haired man named Barth. "We must all learn to be more *contemporary*," she urged.

Frank had lunch with her every day, hung around her office, drove her to her apartment in bad weather, talked her into joining him and his students at The Cave. But she was always anxious to get home, to relieve her babysitter and to work on her classroom preparations; she was so serious! At times Frank's patient grin began to ache, waiting for her to get through with all this seriousness and talk of literature and "relevance". . . . They sat crowded together in pub booths, arguing and complimenting each other; from time to time a sharp, almost searing glance flashed between them, and Frank would feel a little dizzy with certainty. . . . But

68

always she had to get home, always she was gathering up her big leather purse and striding away, and he would be left with his gaggle of students.

At home, he sat in his study, in his big black leather chair, and thought about Molly. His wife's comfortable, bovine presence annoyed him; even his boys distracted him from his dreams of Molly. Sometimes he went out late at night, saying he needed cigarettes (he had begun smoking again, after meeting Molly, breaking his five-year period of abstinence); he telephoned Molly to ask how she was. She always said, "Very busy! My head is whirling, I have so much to do! But I love it." Frank could not decide if she was being deliberately coy. She really confused him. So he would ask if she needed any help, if she needed a mature, male viewpoint ... he would be glad to drop in. ...

But she always said, "No thanks! It's very thoughtful of you, though."

As the winter deepened and the Ontario sky became perpetually smudged, pressing low upon the spirit, even Molly began to slow down. Frank noticed that her stride was not quite so energetic, and one of his colleagues commented zestfully: "It looks like Molly is coming in for a landing, like the rest of us." Frank took her out for coffee and asked her if anything was wrong. She wore an outfit that seemed to be made of green burlap, hanging dramatically about her and highlighting her small, serious face.

"Well, I've been working very hard this semester," she said slowly. "I have so many student compositions to correct ... I'm way behind on my dissertation. ..."

"Anything else?"

Molly hesitated. "Well, I'm having trouble with my ex-husband. He's trying to get out of the child-support payments. He is such a bastard, you wouldn't know. ... Or, yes, maybe you would know," she said, raising her eyes dramatically to Frank.

They were sitting in a small, grimy coffee shop; Frank dared public attention and patted her hand. It was a very small, delicate, pale hand, and the sight of his own dark hand on it pleased him, excited him.

"Maybe I would know, yes," he said, wondering what he meant by this.

"You and I understand each other. We have so much in common, so much. . . ." Molly said, her large brown eyes filling with tears. "Oh, sometimes I could scream, this whole university is filled with fossils who don't *understand*, they just don't *understand*. . . ."

And then, as if she'd confessed too much, she hurried away to a class. Frank was left sitting there, stunned, wondering if he was falling in love.

Obviously, he had never been in love before.

She avoided him for several days after this; he asked her to lunch and their conversation was interrupted by the intrusion of the Department's would-be poet, Ron Blass. He called her one evening when his wife was at a meeting of the Faculty Wives Association, told her he had something to say to her, and talked her into letting him come over.

"All right," she said reluctantly, "but give me time to put Jimmy to bed . . . he hasn't been feeling well. . . ."

When he got there he was a little disappointed at the way her apartment was furnished. "I'm trying to live within my means," she said dryly. She offered him a drink, though, and Frank smiled happily. He believed he could feel how dazzling his smile was.

"Let's talk," he said. "Are you happy here?"

"Yes. No. Not really," she said.

Such a pretty young woman, in spite of the circles of fatigue under her eyes! She wore black net stockings of a diamond design that made Frank lose track of the conversation now and then. She was complaining about her ex-husband, and then about the heavy teaching load. "But, Frank, this job means more to me than anything right now. Thank God you people hired me! So many universities turned me down . . . I was getting desperate. . . . My son has this allergy problem I told you about, and I don't have medical coverage for him, and I was really getting panicked. . . . I think that some English departments wouldn't hire me because of my appearance, maybe, or my views on things," she said, looking Frank in the eye as if he might not believe so bizarre a statement. Frank nodded slowly. "And of course there's the male chauvinism to fight. . . . God, what a fight it's going to be! Centuries of discrimination and prejudice. . . . Men have got to be re-educated if it destroys them."

She stared down at her polished nails and her several big, metallic rings. Frank wondered my she had referred to men as "them" in his presence, as if she weren't talking to a man. . . . This was strange.

"Have men exploited you very much?" Frank asked.

"God, yes."

He got up and came to sit beside her. She laughed bitterly.

"Why don't you tell me about it?" he said in a gentle voice.

"Thank you, but I'm not a self-pitying woman. Thank you anyway," she said, drawing back from him. "But you know what it's like."

"What it's like—?"

"To be discriminated against."

Frank stared at her.

"What's wrong?" she said.

Frank began to stammer. "Just what—what did you mean by that statement—Would you kindly explain that statement?"

"What statement?"

"That I—I'm supposed to know—Supposed to know what it's like to be discriminated against—"

"Well, don't you?" Molly asked. "Being a black, you've been treated like dirt by the white male Establishment—haven't you? Haven't they victimized you? Blacks and women are both—"

Frank could not believe his ears. He grabbed her arm.

"Well, we didn't get together tonight to talk about that kind of stuff," he said hotly, and as she tugged away from him he felt his accent slipping, growing richer, thicker, "there's anything I hate it's a woman who talks too much—"

"What? You're crazy!"

"*You're* crazy!" Frank yelled. A flame seemed to burn in his brain, he was so angry. "Look, you been givin' me the eye now for

71

four months an' I been tailin' around after you as if I got nothin' better to do, when Jesus Christ there are little girls waiting in line —*I mean waiting in line*, sister—so don't hand me none of this crap—"

Molly jumped to her feet. She yanked his pale yellow ascot out of his shirt and up onto his face, so that he was blinded for a second.

"Get the hell out of here! Go home to your honky wife!" she cried.

He went home, furious. He was never to speak to her again.

For weeks he went around muttering to himself, avoiding Molly in the hall, avoiding even his students. When a red-haired freshman dropped in to chat with him about the "erotic symbolism of T. S. Eliot," he did not trust his assessment of her sweet little smiles. No, he couldn't trust his judgment. Was the girl really smiling so deeply at him. . . . ? Or was he being fooled again?

One day Frank put on his neatest, grayest suit, asked the Head of the Department, Dr. Barth, to call an emergency meeting of the Appointments & Promotion Committee, and explained in a terse, quiet voice that his "special relationship" with the student body allowed him to know things that the rest of the Department did not know.

"The students have no respect for Miss Holt," he said sadly. "They laugh at her—evidently she mispronounces words. She doesn't prepare her lectures. I've overheard her talking with students in the coffee shop and she actually gives them misinformation—it's just pathetic, unbelievable—I've put off telling you this because the situation is so ugly. But it was on my strong recommendation that she was hired last year, and it's my responsibility now to tell you what is going on. . . ."

"No complaints about her have come to me," Dr. Barth said slowly.

"The students are reluctant to talk to you, Dr. Barth," Frank said, "because you're—well, you're so obviously above their trivial problems, so they think. They come to me because there's—well, I suppose less of an age difference—"

Dr. Barth nodded gravely. "Yes, I know I'm out of touch with this generation. I know. But about Miss Holt: there may be trouble dismissing her. She's going to be awarded a Ph.D. from Chicago, after all. . . ."

"No, she hasn't been working on her dissertation all year," Frank said. "I don't know what she's been doing. Actually, I wonder about her professional commitment. . . ."

The other members of the committee murmured agreement.

Frank went on solemnly, "It comes down to the preservation of our professional standards. We cannot afford," he said, looking from face to face, "in this time of disintegrating values, to have so casual and uncommitted a teacher in our department. Miss Holt is just not respected by her students. Evidently she refers to the rest of us, in her classes, as *fossils*."

"Fossils . . . ?"

"I told you it was an ugly situation," Frank said softly.

Dr. Barth called a special meeting of the entire department for Monday morning. Molly came in late and Frank did no more than glance at her, nervously. She pulled out a chair at the far end of the big oval table everyone was seated around, and the giddiness of her outfit—really, she had gone too far, wearing a loose-knit black tunic over violet jersey pants to school!—seemed to show everyone how hopeless she was. Dr. Barth began the meeting in his usual grim, paternal voice, his hands clasped in front of him. He spoke of unpleasant reports, of an unfortunate situation, of the rigorous standards of this particular department, etc., etc. He was the only one who was looking at Molly, who in her turn was glancing around, curiously. Frank stared at his own manicured fingernails. His heart raced. Why, the old man sounded so sorry for her, was he going to change his mind? Maybe just reprimand her?

Dr. Barth said, "Because of special circumstances, the Committee on Appointments and Promotions has been forced to suggest that the contract of Miss Holt be not renewed for next year. This decision was reached after many hours of anguish, after many, many hours of discussion. . . . There are budget problems, also, which might involve our slightly reducing the salaries of other department members, unless the lectureship held by Miss Holt is terminated. But this should in no way, of course, influence your vote on the matter. Under the terms of our by-laws I have therefore called this meeting of the department to request that you support the committee's recommendation and terminate Miss Holt's contract. . . ."

Molly was gaping at him.

"What . . . ?" she said faintly.

No one dared look at her. Many of the department members had been told by Dr. Barth of the reason for the meeting; the others stared at one another in disbelief.

Molly, sitting so pertly at the far end of the table, seemed suddenly to shrink.

"But why. . . . ? What are the reasons . . . ? Can't I defend myself . . . ?"

"Under the terms of our university by-laws," Dr. Barth said gently, "no reasons for non-renewal of contract need be stated. Only in the case of non-renewal of a tenured faculty member need reasons be given."

"But I. . . . I don't understand. . . ."

Frank glanced down at her. That small, pale face! That white bitch!

"If you would like to say anything, I'm sure we would all listen with sympathy," Dr. Barth said.

"I. . . . I. . . ."

She fell silent.

After a minute or so Dr. Barth said, "Then we really should get on with the vote. . . . Some of us have eleven o'clock classes we must teach."

Stiff white slips of paper were passed around for the vote.

Frank scribbled *Dismissal* on his ballot at once, folded it neatly in two and then in two again.

Next to him sat old Miss Snyder, a back-number from the university's really mediocre years; with her billowing gray dresses and her stern, medieval nose, she had always disliked Molly Holt. No problem there. On Frank's left was the poet, Blass, who kept shifting miserably in his seat. Around the large, highly polished table everyone sat in silence, staring down at their ballots. They seemed reluctant to vote. The only people who sat with their heads up were Frank and Dr. Barth and Molly, whose ballot lay before her, untouched.

"Really, we must hurry. . . . It's quarter to eleven," Dr. Barth said.

The ballots were collected by the departmental secretary and counted out. Frank could overhead the count: *For* dismissal. *Against* dismissal. He began to sweat, wondering if he might lose. *What if . . . ? What if . . . ?* What if that bitch had managed to win her way into the hearts of the other professors, what if she'd told them the same hard-luck story she had told him? What if they refused to believe him . . . ? His nostrils flared. In that case he would quit. Would quit. Would quit with dignity. Yes, he would quit. He would not remain in this department if his professional integrity was doubted. . . .

Dr. Barth anounced the results: "The vote is 16 to 5 for non-renewal of Miss Holt's contract."

Molly pushed her chair back clumsily and got to her feet. "But I . . . I still don't understand. . . ."

"I will be happy to talk with you and to make suggestions about where you might apply for a new position," Dr. Barth said at once. "In fact, we would be all happy to help you. . . ."

Molly snatched up her big leather purse and hurried out of the room.

Relief.

Frank lingered with some of the others, shaking his head gravely as they shook theirs. He had to admit he'd been taken in by her . . . he had to admit he'd made a mistake. . . . The whole ugly mess was his fault, he said.

"No, don't blame yourself, Frank," everyone said.

Dr. Barth patted his arm. "Frank, we belong to a profession with extremely rigorous standards. Personal feelings shouldn't enter into it at all. I'm sure Miss Holt will be happier in another university, with less demanding criteria of excellence. . . ."

But Frank found it difficult to be comforted. He felt really down. Instead of going out to The Cave with his students that afternoon, he went right home. His wife was frightened by his dour, peevish frown.

"You're not sick, Frank. . . . ?"

No, not sick. He put on his smoking jacket and went to sit in his leather chair, he wanted to be alone. Eunice opened his study door to ask, meekly, if he wanted dinner delayed. "Yes. Maybe an hour," he said. She then asked if the twins could come play with him for a few minutes—they'd been waiting for him to come home all day.

Frank considered this.

His eye travelled up from his excellent shoes to his slim, checked trousers to the casual richness of his navy blue smoking jacket. He had knotted a white ascot quickly around his neck. He sensed his totality, his completion—a man who did not need anyone else, certainly not a woman. *Not that white bitch. Not any white bitch at all.* But he had lived through a certain draining emotional experience —there was little doubt in his mind that it had been an experience —and though he had triumphed as he had known he would, still he felt a little melancholy. It was a delicate, sensitive, almost poetic melancholy, and his twin boys were so healthy and noisy that they might destroy it.

So he said, "No, not right now. I want to be alone. I feel a little melancholy and I want to be alone for a while."

A DESCRIPTIVE CATALOGUE

It began with an eerie casualness—the most unpleasant semester the English Department had yet endured. Though later events would follow one another with a rigid, merciless logic, a kind of scholarly precision, the initial event was certainly an accident.

On an ordinary Tuesday morning in January, Ron Blass was in his office, the door open as usual, having a conference with a student from his Poetry Workship. The girl was friendly and eager and handed in to Ron several times a week extremely frank, even clinical verse about the problems of being a young woman "liberated" but only to a certain degree—so Ron was careful to keep the door wide open, since he did not want the girl to misunderstand his interest in her. Though he was a short, rather stocky man in his mid-thirties, whose pale brown hair had thinned sadly, and whose face was comfortable and lived-in, rather than dramatic, there were still a few girl students, from time to time, who were attracted to him. He was married, more or less happily, and even when his marriage swayed, when the arguments with his wife increased, he somehow kept a faith in the Platonic promise of marriage: if not his own, always, then the idea of marriage itself. Also, he liked his students too much to want to hurt them; even when they handed in atrocious work—like this girl's raw, mawkish verse, so unskillful that it must not even have been plagiarized—Ron had too easygoing and gentle a disposition to criticize them. He was very friendly by nature, gregarious and talkative, and dreaded the idea of criticizing anyone at all.

So the door to his office was open, and through the door walked another professor—Reynold Mason—who had yanked a sheet of paper or a letter out of a manila envelope and was reading it, frowning, his head bent, so that he hadn't known he was walking into Ron's office instead of his own. Though Mason was only a year or two older than Ron he was a little absent-minded, and this was the second time he'd walked into Ron's office this year; his own office was next door. He glanced up from the letter, saw Ron and the girl staring at him, and flushed deeply. He stammered an apology, saying that he hadn't looked where he was going—he was sorry to interrupt—he was—he thought— But the girl, who was extremely cheerful that morning, burst into appreciative laugher. She shook her head, making her short bouncy curls shake, her eyes narrowed to slits, saying, "You guys really are funny—like in cartoons or something—all that stuff is really true!" And she laughed, so heartily and innocently that Ron himself had to join in. He expected Mason to laugh with them, at least to smile, but Mason just stood there staring, staring as if struck, the flush now spread out across his face and into his throat. His embarrassment turned into anger: he muttered something about manners, about rudeness, about ugly fat girls who belonged in cartoons themselves.

Then he walked out. Ron was more surprised than the girl; he had been really startled, jolted, by the viciousness of Mason's words.

"He didn't mean it—he's under a terrible strain—he hasn't been himself lately," Ron said, as the girl sat with one hand pressed against her face, staring at the empty doorway. "Dr. Mason is up for tenure—I think—I think that's his problem—and he's worried about being kept on here—I think—that *must* be his problem— I'm sure the situation could be explained—I mean—there must be an explanation," Ron finished lamely.

The girl grabbed her books and walked out.

After that, Ron began to notice that Reynold Mason behaved oddly toward him. If they met outside the Humanities Building, or in any area where no other colleagues or students were near, Mason just ignored him; he walked as quickly as he could, past Ron. If they met when other faculty members were around, Mason would look at Ron in a mock-admiring way and ask how his work was going—He must have a second book of poems to be published, didn't he?—since the first had been published so long ago?—and was there any current work of his in magazines, so that he, Reynold Mason, could read it? "I'm very envious of poets," Mason said. "I know they lead fascinating lives."

Ron licked his lips, and replied that he was gathering poems for a second book, and that he'd be happy to show Mason his new work—yes certainly— He was so defenseless, in his black sweater and wide-buckled belt and blue jeans, with an inexpensive copper medallion on a leather thong around his neck, that even Mason sometimes pitied him and withdrew from the attack. If he walked out, and the others remained there, embarrassed, Ron laughed nervously and said, "Well, he's nervous about losing his job," or, ". . . he's nervous about the student evaluations this week," or ". . . he puts too much emphasis on publication and is, maybe is a little jealous. . . ."

Ron was the most frequently-published member of the Department: a mimeographed newsletter was brought out each month, and the column that dealt with publications was always dominated by Ron's bibliography. He listed poems by their full titles, which were sometimes rather long, and he sometimes spaced these titles in his paragraph so that it was necessary to repeat the name of the magazine in which they appeared; if he did book reviews for the local newspaper, he was careful to give the full title and the name of the author of the book reviewed; he listed the readings he did at the local pub, which had poetry readings open to everyone on Friday evenings, and since he had a ten-minute program on the university's radio station each Saturday morning, he was careful to give the name of his talk. But he really did publish poetry widely—in little-known magazines like *Sink, Scorpion, The Ork Review, Druids*

Choice, and *Rejects.* He was personally modest about being so prolific, but always included in the biographical information that accompanied his poems an exact count of his publications up to that
time: he had begun this semester with a record of 358 poems
published in 53 magazines or newspapers in Canada, the United
States, England, Wales, and Australia.

No one else in the English Department could approach him, in
terms of sheer quantity of publications. A very poor second was
Dr. Barth, the chairman of the Department himself, who listed as
publications certain mimeographed memos sent to the university
senate, or speeches made at PTA meetings in the area, as well as
his frequent brief contributions to the *Burke Newsletter* and *Minor
Augustans,* which were both edited by ex-students of his. In third
place, possibly, was Dr. Robinson Thayer, a Renaissance specialist
who had written several important books as a young man but who,
in recent years, only published brief notes attacking other
scholars' discoveries; Thayer's reputation was above reproach,
however, since he was a full professor with tenure. A few other
colleagues published articles or papers or notes occasionally—
Miss Snyder, a medievalist, and Dr. May, a Victorian drama specialist. Reynold Mason, hired on the strength of his having worked
with Northrop Frye at the University of Toronto, had managed so
far to place only two essays—on the savage critical response to
William Blake's only private exhibition of fresco-paintings, and on
Blake's concept of heroic painting, as set forth in his *Descriptive
Catalogue.* Both appeared in excellent scholarly journals, but
since that time—and it had been several years now—Mason had not
published at all. In fact, it had become something of a departmental joke—his pacing the corridors before the mail deliveries at
10 A.M. and 2 P.M., distracted, anxious, ghostly. There was an aura,
almost a physical smell, of fear and yearning about him. . . .

He must be jealous of me, Ron thought. At first he was surprised,
then he was amused; then he began to worry. He stopped telling his
wife about the peculiar mumbled remarks Mason made in the Common Room, or in the men's lavatory, or as they passed on the
stairs—often when Ron was trooping along with a group of stu-

dents, all of them chuckling and joking around, after Ron's writing workshops or his big Canadian literature class, which was very popular. Though Ron Blass had only an M.A. degree from Edmonton, he had been promoted to the rank of Associate Professor with tenure ahead of Reynold Mason and others who had joined Hilberry's staff at the same time—the reason being, as Dr. Barth said, that the Department could recognize creative talent when it was so obvious, and that they were all impressed with Ron's productivity and the great numbers of students who enrolled in his courses. Along with the department's only black man, Ron received near-perfect scores in the yearly student evaluation reports that were published by the university. *I have to expect people to be jealous,* Ron told himself.

But he began to get a little frightened. If he walked into the Common Room to get some coffee, it sometimes happened that Reynold Mason was in there, reading something to a few giggling graduate students, in his cold, sarcastic, beautifully-modulated voice—and if Ron allowed himself to look at what Mason had, it might turn out to be a copy of *Scorpion* or *Rejects*, in which Ron had a few poems. When he checked the library's *Canadian Literature, Contemporary* shelf, where three copies of his book of poems were usually to be found, he discovered all three copies annotated with exclamation points, question marks, sarcastic scrawls that seemed to say, in Mason's voice, *Oh! Ah? Really?* and other words he didn't dare decipher. He felt sick at heart, baffled. It was impossible to apologize to Mason because he had really done nothing wrong—nothing that made sense. In fact, it was Ron who was being injured, and Reynold Mason who owed him an apology. So Ron didn't know what to do. He began to dread seeing Mason's tall, angular figure in the hall or coming accidentally upon him in the men's room—where Mason was often to be found, dabbing at his face with wet paper towels, as if he were warm or nervous before his classes. If Ron encountered him at these time he met Ron's startled gaze boldly and defiantly in the mirror above the sink: Mason was almost a handsome man, but his features had grown thin and puckered, and his head had an unfortunate wedge-shaped appearance which he seemed to emphasize, unconsciously, by a habit he had of drawing his neck up and out from his shoulders. He was only thirty-seven but looked much older: he even wore white shirts, and ordinary neckties.

Ron knew that the situation had become dangerous when Mason turned up one evening at the Hilberry Pub, to sit alone in the midst of the noisy cheerful audience of undergraduates and graduate students, staring at Ron while he read his newest poems. Ron had had a bit to drink, so it wasn't too bad, and he managed to laugh away the disturbance Mason caused by standing abruptly and pushing his way out, saying *Excuse me!* in a loud voice.

But he knew it would happen soon: he would be attacked.

The attack came unexpectedly, a full two months after the morning Mason had walked absent-mindedly into Ron't office. The department was meeting in order to discuss curriculum and calendar changes for the following year, and at the meeting there were student representatives and an Assistant Dean of Humanities in addition to the regular staff. But before Dr. Barth could even call for a vote of approval of the minutes for the previous meeting, Reynold Mason put his hand up. He said, "Dr. Barth, excuse me," and cleared his throat nervously, getting to his feet, with an abruptness that startled everyone. Mason was wearing a new suit, and very handsome and costly it appeared, but his face was a strange mixture of pallor and red blotches or rashes. He seemed to be addressing Dr. Barth personally, but he spoke in a loud, careful voice. "I am requesting, Dr. Barth, the immediate naming of a committee, a committee comprised of the department's senior staff, in order to investigate and expose—to further investigate—to further expose— the charges of gross plagiarism, gross and willful and absurd and possibly criminal plagiarism that I am bringing against—I, Reynold Mason, am hereby bringing against one Ronald Blass, Associate Professor in our department. I request—I must insist—"

Dr. Barth was a gentle, white-haired man in his sixties, and he was too surprised to rule Mason out of order. Dean Harr said, "Dr. Mason, please, this is hardly the place—hardly the time—"

"I accuse him of willful and gross plagiarism, possibly criminal

84

plagiarism," Mason said in a quivering voice. "I will back my accusation with evidence—"

"Dr. Mason—"

"—evidence resulting from my meticulous research—cross-references—two months' labor—analyzing literature of the most asinine and illiterate sort—*Snork* and *Snark* and American beat poets of the Fifties—not to mention minor poems by Lawrence and Samuel Gregory and H. D.—"

Ron, who was sitting at the rear of the room, near the door, got slowly to his feet and walked out.

It had happened.

He drove out to a tavern overlooking Lake Ontario, where no one knew him. When he came home, at two in the morning, he was drunk, sick, disheveled, tearful, and he collapsed in his wife's arms on the front porch of their house.

He stayed away from the university for a week, locked upstairs in his study. Dr. Barth's secretary called several times, but Ron refused to speak to her. He sat at his work-desk, which he had cleared of all papers, staring at nothing, at his hands, while again and again Reynold Mason's voice rose in his mind. *I accuse . . . I accuse. . . .* He even slept in his study, telling his wife that he had to be alone. He couldn't face her or their two small children. She knew what had happened at the meeting, from other sources, and she was sometimes sympathetic with him, but at other times furious: "Sleep alone the rest of your life, then," she would say, sneering, "you and your poetry!"

Finally he answered the telephone. The secretary informed him that Dr. Barth and Dean Harr had named a committee to investigate his case—his "case"—and that the committee requested he appear before them as soon as possible. So he agreed, hollowly. He agreed. He knew they were going to fire him, it was going to happen, and not even his wife's angry tears could awaken him from a heavy, lethargic trance. "I knew we should never have left Edmonton," Marcella wept. "And we owe $11,000 on the mortgage and we might have to sell the house to anyone, at any price—my God, Ron, how could you do this to your own family?"

The first hearing lasted several hours. It was held in Dr. Barth's inner office, and though it was a secret, closed meeting, somehow a number of people seemed to know about it. Ron, his face weakly composed, had to make his way through a jostling crowd of students who clutched at him as he passed, saying *Is it true?* and *We won't let them get you, Ron!* A photographer from the Hilberry *Cardinal* took half a dozen pictures of him, and he had to resist shielding his face with his hands, like a criminal entering a courthouse.

The committee consisted of Dr. Barth and Dean Harr, three senior professors, and Reynold Mason himself. After an embarrassed, rambling preliminary speech by Dr. Barth, who avoided looking directly at Ron, the meeting was given over to Mason. He spoke briskly and clearly, without a trace of his usual sarcasm, reading the details of his findings on the "case." Before him on the table was a pile of papers; he glanced up often as he read, but never looked directly at Ron. His presentation began with the textual analysis he had done of the forty-five poems in Ron's first book, *many gods*, published by the Small Cellar Press in Toronto, some years ago. Most of these early poems, Mason stated, "*are* original with Mr. Blass, and the only overt plagiarism one might discern is self-plagiarism. That is, Mr. Blass repeats himself endlessly. However, when we consider the three hundred—or is it more?—the three hundred-odd poems Mr. Blass claims to have written since the publication of the book, we soon discover outright borrowings—the actual theft of lines and, in the case of 'Ecstasy,' a short poem published in *Titmouse Review*, we see how the poet has deliberately transposed and distorted an already unintelligible poem by the American poet Allen Ginsberg—I believe he is an American poet? Is he, Mr. Blass?"

Ron, who had ben staring blankly at Mason, did not hear the question and Mason had to repeat it.

From Ginsberg to Lawrence, from Lawrence to H. D., from H. D. to Yeats—"Yeats himself!" Mason exclaimed—and back again, page after page of evidence, lines from a poem "by Ron Blass" cruelly and horribly compared to lines from other poems, a maze of cross-references that left Ron bewildered, empty, sick. He sat facing the committee, and he saw how they were assessing him, surreptitiously, dismissing the feeble composure of his face, concentrating upon the damp pallor of his skin and the queer tension in his jaws. He had to keep his jaws rigid, upper and lower teeth set harsh together, or he might shriek. And that would be the end of him.

As Mason continued his exposé Ron's mind wandered, as if detaching itself from that cool, relentless voice. He knew he was doomed: the only person in the room who sympathized with him was Dr. Barth, but Barth's position was hopeless. He was not even looking at Ron. He had always taken such pride in Ron, had congratulated him on his big enrollments every semester, had praised their "poet-in-residence"—and now Ron had betrayed him. And Barth had no real friends on this committee. Dean Harr was an ex-member of the Classics Department, an old, stern, but rather confused-looking man, a friend of Heva Snyder, who was sitting beside him, Dr. Snyder with her metallic, medieval face—looking so bluntly and so coldly at Ron's feet. Today he was wearing regular shoes, not boots or sandals. But she stared coldly at him just the same. Dr. Snyder had disagreed with Dr. Barth on a number of important issues in the past several years—she had fought bitterly to prevent the easing of requirements in the Old and Middle English Language area, and, having returned from a sabbatical spent at the Medieval Institute in Toronto, she had demanded her former, spacious office back, in vain—so it was hopeless, hopeless. She would never be sympathetic with Ron. She and Dean Harr were old friends: unmarried, they often accompanied one another to university functions, and had worked up several violin-and-piano pieces together. Ron himself had heard them play once, years ago. And today they were joined in silent, crotchety opposition to him, as if he had offended them somehow simply by existing.

Next to Heva Snyder sat Dr. Thayer, Robinson Thayer, a Renaissance scholar whose hair was cut brutally short and whose small, shrewd, malicious gaze was fastened on Ron's tense mouth. Ron dared not lick his lips, aware of Dr. Thayer staring at him. Thayer had never liked him—evidently he did not like, or even know by name, the "new people," those who had joined the staff in the last ten or fifteen years. He wore a dark green, a very dark green suit, a muddy-brown green tweed suit, with an olive-black necktie; his manner was fastidious and detached. In fact, he hardly seemed to be listening to Reynold Mason's lengthy exposé. From time to time he broke his gaze away from Ron to swing it over onto Mason himself, contemptuously, and then briefly onto Dr. Barth, who sat staring down at a collection of notecards before him. According to departmental tradition there was a long-standing feud between Dr. Thayer and Dr. Barth: Ron had heard from some sources that Thayer despised Barth because Barth's only published book, *Satire and Lyricism in Charles Churchill*, contained a footnote praising a Cambridge scholar who had, sometime in his career, presented a very convincing case for the claim of the playwright Middleton, as opposed to Middleton's contemporary, Sturgess, regarding some fragments of a manuscript . . . but Ron had also heard that the feud began when Dr. Barth had attempted to talk to Dr. Thayer about the many complaints he had been receiving from students in Thayer's classes. . . . It was a hopeless, confused tangle. Ron knew that Thayer would never support him or Barth: in fact, Thayer had not spoken to Dr. Barth for several years, communicating with him only through memos and formal letters addressed to Head, Department of English, and given to Barth's secretary.

The fifth member of the committee, Basil May, was a tense youngish man in his forties, rather like Mason in manner—abrupt, elegant, witty—though he was more confident than Mason, having recently published a critical work with Oxford University Press, *Dynamics of Neutrals: Black, White, and Gray Imagery in "The Ring and the Book"*; it had received an excellent notice in the *Times Literary Supplement* and portions of that review had appeared in the department newsletter last fall. Dr. May, whose degrees were all from Toronto, had last spoken to Ron many months before, and then vaguely and perfunctorily, when Ron had happened to meet him in the branch bank near the university. All these people, Ron thought, were scholars in English Literature: they despised Canadian Literature, and, unable to speak out against it, they concentrated their disgust on people like Ron himself, poets, "poets," and hardly shared Dr. Barth's disappointment—they were really delighted. He could feel it, their delight. From time to time Heva Snyder blew her nose angrily, when Reynolds Mason made an especially damaging point, and Basil May nodded impatiently, murmuring *yes, yes,* as if he had really guessed this all along.

May interrupted Mason in the midst of his reading of a poem by the Canadian poet Sam Gregory—a poet of the Forties, now dead— saying with an unmistakable excitement: "But—Dr. Mason!— don't you know what you're reading?"

Mason looked up at him, startled. "I beg your pardon?"

"Don't you—yourself—know what you are reading?"

Mason squirmed. He stretched his neck as if his shirt collar were very uncomfortable. He said, hesitantly, "I'm reading a poem called 'Heavenly Haven,' written by Samuel Gregory in . . . let's see . . . 1941 . . . and the point I am attempting to make, which I believe I have already made, is that it bears a curious resemblance . . . I mean, an *exactness,* to Mr. Blass's 'Haven of Green,' which appeared in a recent issue of *Hearse.* I think the committee will agree—"

"That's not my point at all, not at all," May said. He even smiled at Mason. "Finish reading the poem, please."

Mason obeyed him at once, like a student. He read the poem in a rapid, nervous voice, "*I wanted to go/where life does not fail/ to fields without flies and hail/and a few lilies blow . . . . And I wanted to be/Where no tides come/Where flowers in the haven dumb/And out of the smell of the sea. . . .* My point is, I mean, it seems to me obvious that, that Mr. Blass was deliberately plagiarizing from Samuel Gregory, in his version which I'll read again:

     i'm going
        where climates don't fail

```
        fields fly-filled OK
        curdled lilies OK
   i'm going
                    into the tides
                    into the smell
           of
              the
 sea.
```

Now isn't that—isn't that a direct plagiarism?" Mason asked.

"But you seem to be entirely unaware," May said, "astonishingly unaware, of an early, obscure poem of Hopkins, written sometime in the years 1865-1866, called 'Heaven-Haven,' which is about a nun taking the veil. We are certainly impressed with your ability to scout back to 1941, Dr. Mason, but it might seem that anyone who had studied with Northrop Frye himself might have a more flexible, a more scholarly sense of the *tradition* that dates back beyond even our precious Samuel Gregory. . . . Let me see, I'm not a Hopkins scholar at all, but perhaps I can remember that poem. . . ." He paused for a few seconds, frowning carefully, then recited: "*I have desired to go/Where springs not fail,/To fields where flies no sharp and sided hail/And a few lilies blow./And I have asked to be/Where no storms come,/Where the green swell is in the havens dumb,/And out of the swing of the sea.*"

The committee sat in silence, and Dean Harr glanced nervously at Dr. Barth. What a brilliant man! What a brilliant performance! Reynold Mason, licking his lips, waited for a while as if expecting Dr. May to give him permission to continue. But May, having made his point, now sat back, relaxed, in such a mood of well-being that he actually smiled with half of his mouth at Ron. Ron felt too lethargic, too empty, to respond.

"How very . . . very interesting. . . . How strange . . . yes, and and . . . and interesting," Dr. Barth said feebly. He was not a subtle man, but vaguely well-meaning, so he could not have known how cruel his remark was to Ron, when he asked him, in a gentle voice, which poet he had "consulted"?—Gregory or Hopkins?

Ron stammered that he could not remember.

"... oh yes, yes, I suppose ... yes, that might well be the case," Barth said sadly. "Do you remember writing the poem at all, Ron?"

"I ... I ... I.... I don't remember," Ron said miserably. He paused. "Yes. I do remember. I guess I do. I...."

Here followed a very long pause. The committee waited, embarrassed, but Ron just could not think of anything to say. He sat there, staring at the floor. But the moment was saved by Dr. Thayer, who brought his fist down violently on the table before him, and said, "Ha! Hopkins, eh? That fruity alliterative maniac, *that* popish torturer of words—Hopkins, is it?—*you* may think so," he said, though he did not turn to address Dr. May, who sat beside him, "yes, you may well think so, since your knowledge of English Literature no doubt crumples weirdly when one pursues you along the maze that pre-dates even your precious Victorian era ... a stew of rabble shrieking and puling for more democracy.... I would not dare compete, Dr. May, with your theatrical *coup*, though I should like to refresh the committee's somewhat mysteriously eroded memory by calling to their attention Sturgess's *A Humorous Day's Mirth*, produced by the Admiral's Men in March 1597, in which we see quite clearly—nay, unmistakably—the roots of an entire tradition."

Dr. May began to speak, then thought better of it. Dr. Barth said, hesitantly, "Perhaps we might continue the matter under discussion.... It's such a difficult, tense issue, involving, as you know, so many of us ... indirectly.... It is not just a need to seek out the truth, I mean, I mean it is also ... a requirement ... the committee should address itself to ... certain human considerations.... And also, also ... certain public considerations...."

"Dr. Barth means that this entire issue will make the English Department, and the University itself, look rather foolish," Dean Harr said. He had seemed rather confused during most of Mason's presentation, but now he spoke clearly. "Last year the case of Dr. Bird was publicized everywhere in Ontario, and—"

"Ah!" Dr. Thayer interrupted. "Does not the bow, bent and drawn, make from the shaft? Or have times so changed, so stooped to folly, that, under the guidance of Dr. Barth, the essential truth of the matter will be obscured?"

"Dr. Thayer—"

He rose, briskly. He seemed very angry and yet pleased. Ron knew that Thayer had always disliked him, and had seemed to approve of Dr. May, and even of Dr. Mason, but now he smiled at them all in the same contemptuous way. "I refuse to be a party to this absurd investigating committee—so totally lacking in ferocity and daring—as usual—it simply takes too much faith in our present mode of administrative government to believe that anything other than nothing can come from nothing: it's a lesson I have learned well, in my twenty-three years at this university." He went to the door, turned back to them, and said in a heavily-ironic voice, emphasizing each word, *"Nothing will come from nothing."*

". . . *of* nothing," May said suddenly.

Thayer left the room.

For a few moments they sat, quiet. Dean Harr whispered with Dr. Snyder, then leaned over to confer with Dr. Barth. Barth said, in a voice not meant to be audible, ". . . very hard-working . . . his lectures, you know . . . prepares ten hours, they say . . . for each lecture. . . . *very* highly-thought-of. . . . Oxford . . . tenure . . . . valuable. . . . scholarship. . . . Tenure."

The meeting was turned over to Mason again, but he had no more begun his final point, 25-c on the photostated papers he had passed around, than Dr. Snyder interrupted. "Not Sturgess. Not Sturgess. Someone else—another of those ruffians—someone else— Chapman, it was. *Him.*"

Mason smiled shakily, then continued. But it turned out that this final point was only a somewhat heavy-handed ironic discussion of Ron Blass's brief essay in a recent issue of *Canadian Forum*, called "Poetic Imperialism: Will the U.S. Corrupt Us All?"—the irony being, as Mason said, that Blass had plagiarized freely from a number of American poets.

"However, that essay was well-received," Dr. Barth said. "A number of high-school teachers in the area. . . . liked it very much."

"However," Dr. May said irritably, "that has nothing to do with Dr. Mason's argument."

Ron looked at his watch and saw that an hour and a half had passed. He wondered if he could survive much longer. The thought of being free of this torture—somewhere far away—in one of the roadhouses out along the lake—the thought of a can of beer—a fistful of salty peanuts—He felt almost faint. With an effort he tried to respond to Dr. Barth's questions, put to him in a kindly, embarrassed way. His voice was the voice of a guilty man. No disguising it. No way out. He heard his voice say, "... I ... I must have done it ... them ... the poems ... must have done them unconsciously...."

Unconsciously. The word hung there for a few seconds. May made a noise that might have been a snicker. Dr. Barth, however, said hopefully, "Well, unconscious art ... automatic writing, is it? ... some of the students do that, I believe ... the *Cardinal* publishes poems of that nature. ... Unconscious, unconscious. ... The mind does strange things, they say, when it is unconscious. It might be possible for a sensitive man, a highly-imaginative and intuitive individual ... a poet ... to somehow...."

"It is not possible," Heva Snyder said bluntly.

Ron closed his eyes.

"... perhaps you have some other explanation?" Dr. Barth asked.

"... I ... I...."

"... perhaps you *were* unconscious? ... at times, I mean ...?"

"... I ... I only ... I only wanted ... I only wanted to...."

"There is a tradition, I believe," Dr. Barth said, in a slow, fumbling voice, "... of what might loosely be called ... plagiarism ... if we must give it a name ... an exact name. ... I believe Coleridge ... and didn't Shakespeare himself ... and, what is her name, the woman who wrote all those poems with the dashes ... the little breathless exclamatory poems. ... I'm very weak on moderns and contemporaries...."

"Emily Dickinson?" Mason said.

"Yes, yes! Didn't she ...? Also ...? My point is just that ... there may be a tradition ... unrecognized ... but perhaps it exists...." But Dr. Barth faltered and was silent.

93

Dean Harr said angrily, "Mr. Blass, explain yourself. *Explain yourself.*"

"I . . . I just don't know . . . I. . . . Something came over me . . . I. . . ."

"*Something came over you!* Three hundred times, did it?—three hundred times?"

Ron felt tears stinging at the corners of his eyes.

"I . . . I wrote lots of poems . . . lots of poems in Edmonton . . . and then, and then I came here . . . I mean, my wife and I and the children moved here . . . and. . . . and something happened. . . ." Ron blinked rapidly, trying to keep his voice from breaking. ". . . Dr. Barth was so nice to me, and I wanted to make him proud of me . . . I wanted the department to be proud of me . . . but . . . but I . . . just discovered, one day I discovered, I just discovered one day when I was doing the shopping for my wife, in the Dominion store on Pelee Blvd., that I . . . I had nothing to say. *I had nothing to say any more.* We bought such a nice house, and . . . and, well, the kids are . . . they're very sweet kids . . . and my students are awfully sweet . . . I love to teach . . . I love it here at Hilberry . . . and. . . And I wanted you all to be proud of me," he said. He began to weep now, helplessly. "Dr. Barth . . . and all of you . . . I wanted you to be proud and, and happy that you had a poet . . . the other universities have poets . . . but Hilberry didn't . . . and . . . and you hired me to be a poet . . . and there was so much pressure to publish . . . things . . . to publish things . . . it could be anything, I thought, because . . . nobody reads it . . . I mean . . . nobody seems to read it. . . . I was so happy here, my teaching and my family and everything made me so happy, oh Dr. Barth, I was so happy, I just didn't have anything more to say. . . . You can't write poems about being happy. . . . Dr. Barth, I only wanted to please you!—you most of all!"

Ron had worked himself into such a state that Dr. Barth adjourned the meeting.

The committee would meet again, in a few weeks, so that Ron would have time to prepare for a more formal defense of his actions. That would give them, Dr. Barth said grimly, "more evidence to consider, before voting."

"Voting—?" Ron asked.

"For or against dismissal," Dr. Barth said.

Dr. Barth's gaze was sorrowful and pink, a look so hurt, so betrayed, that Ron knew he would never forget it.

Though he was very upset, Ron managed to get back to teaching in a few days. But he came to the campus only for his classes, then left immediately. He never went to his office in the Humanities Building. As soon as he finished a class he hurried out of the room, and after a while his students stopped calling after him and following him. At home, he spent most of his time in his study, alone, staring at his work-desk. Nothing lay on it. No more poems, no more writing. He had to begin a formal defense . . . but whenever he thought those words, *formal defense*, his mind panicked. It went empty. He was then nearly overcome by an urge to run out of the house and drive to a roadhouse where no one knew him: there, he could get drunk and plan the restoration of his life. A dozen or more times this urge rose in him, before he gave in.

He was gone for a day, that time.

The next time he stayed away for two days. When he returned, Marcella screamed at him: "What are you doing? What about your defense?"

He told her he would begin it soon: he was gathering strength.

A short while later three graduate students, in Toronto for a weekend, reported that they saw Ron Blass walking on Yonge Street—whether drunk or not, they couldn't say—though when he caught sight of them he ducked into a bookshop. The next weekend, Frank Ambrose's wife, Eunice, shopping on Bloor Street, ran into Ron in a coffee shop—and, after a moment of intense embarrassment, Ron spoke to her in a fairly normal way. But he looked different, she reported: thinner, unsmiling, a little abrupt. He said evasively that he was in Toronto "doing research"—that it was coming along well—but it involved a lot of work and he didn't have time, much as he wished he had, to talk with her. "Then he sort of brushed past me," Eunice said. "He was never like that before."

9 5

One of the assistant professors in the department, a young woman named Wanda, surprised Ron Blass in the Hilberry Library late one Saturday afternoon: he was crouched back in the stacks, with a pile of books around him, muttering to himself. She came upon him by accident, and when he saw her, glancing up at her, he laughed queerly and said, "*You*. I'd forgotten about you." He looked so pale and yet so cheerful that she excused herself, without asking what he meant. Like everyone else, Wanda had heard about the charges brought against Ron, and she wanted nothing to do with him.

Then, one day in mid-April, Ron appeared in the Humanities Building, dressed in his old outfit, a black sweater and jeans and a wide-buckled belt. He went directly to his office, passing by the other offices without glancing inside. He had lost weight but looked well: he had grown a small moustache, which was curly and rather darker than his hair. He carried a large briefcase.

He reappeared, carrying an armful of large, bulky manila envelopes. These he took to the departmental office, where he put them in the mailboxes of a number of his colleagues—sixteen out of the twenty-three members of the full-time teaching staff, the secretary said later. After that he joked with her, though not in the old way, and wandered down the hall to the Common Room, to make himself coffee. He sat in there, his feet up on a bench, and as people came in he glanced up at them, expectantly and alertly. A few of the graduate students hung around, trying to start a conversation with him, but he responded only vaguely, with brief insincere smiles. Then Dr. May came into the room. He and Ron looked at each other. May said falteringly, "Could I . . . could I talk to you? Could you come to my office?"

Ron swung his feet off the bench.

"My office is just down the hall," May said.

In the corridor they ran into Dr. Ambrose, who was just leaving his office, stumbling through the doorway with a confused, stricken look on his face—a handsome black man, but with a look of utter dissolution, an almost ashen alarm. He stared at Ron for a while without seeming to see him. Then he said, "You—Mr. Blass—Ron

—Could I—? Could I talk with you for a minute? Could—?"

"I'm going to talk with him just now," Dr. May said.

"But I—"

"He said he'd talk with me now," May said. "*With me.*"

When the committee met again, in late April, it was already spring; the windows of Dr. Barth's office were opened wide. His secretary had put a vase of forsythia on his desk. He opened the hearing by going over, in a rapid murmur, some of the main points of the previous meeting, but only Reynold Mason seemed to be paying attention. He nodded from time to time, enthusiastically. Dean Harr and Dr. Snyder sat together, as before, but did not look at each other; Dr. Thayer was back, his metallic-gray hair cut very short; Dr. May kept lighting his pipe and re-lighting it, fussing so that he seemed always to be looking down at his hands. Ron, in a pull-over sweater of a light nylon-and-wool material, a new mandala-medallion around his neck, sat facing the committee with his eyes lowered. He looked patient, docile, and yet arrogant. It must have been the new moustache, which was dark brown, and quite curly.

". . . and so . . . and so, I think we can get through this particular meeting quite quickly," Dr. Barth said. "Mr. Blass wishes me to inform the committee that he has prepared no formal defense for himself. Is that correct, Mr. Blass?"

"Yes," Ron said.

". . . no formal defense. Yes. Well, that's too bad," Dr. Barth said, though without paying much attention to his words. "And so. So. I believe we are all ready for the vote . . . ?"

"But shouldn't the charges be read again?" Mason asked.

"Oh yes, yes," Dr. Barth said. He rummaged through a pile of papers and notecards on his desk. He read the charges off, one by one, in a perfunctory voice. "And now . . . you each have paper ballots, I believe? . . . I will reverse the usual procedure and ask you to jot down the word *Yes* if you wish Mr. Blass to be retained here at Hilberry, exactly as before, at the rank he has now, etc., etc., and to write the word *No* if you believe he should be dismissed. No need to bother with the faculty association's by-laws and the circumstances of Mr. Blass's contract . . . I believe we're all fully informed of the situation. . . . Yes, Dr. Mason?"

"But doesn't he have to file some defense?" Mason asked irritably. He looked around at the other committee members. "It might be a trick of his, not to give us any official defense . . . so that later he could claim. . . ."

"Do you intend to make subsequent claims, Mr. Blass?" Dean Harr asked.

"No. I do not."

"But he could go back on his word," Mason protested. "After he's dismissed he could—he could claim—"

"The committee hasn't voted yet," Dr. May said.

"Yes, but—"

"We'll vote now," Dr. Barth said. "Just jot down yes or no—*yes* to keep Mr. Blass on, as before, and *no* if you want dismissal. It's really very simple, Dr. Mason, why make a fuss over it?"

The ballots were passed over to Dr. Barth. He read them off, one by one, and held each up to the group, to demonstrate the openness of the proceeding. "*Yes. Yes. Yes. Yes. No.* And my vote is *Yes*," he said. He smiled at Ron. "Well, Mr. Blass—there you are!"

"*What?*" Mason asked.

"Dr. Mason, the vote is evidently—as you can see—one, two, three, four, five *yeses*, and a single *no*—An almost unanimous decision, quite rare in situations like this," Dr. Barth said.

"But—"

"But the vote is counted now, and quite in order," Dr. Barth said. "I think we should apologize to Mr. Blass, frankly, for having subjected him to so much doubt—and possibly many difficult hours—because of course the strain on Mr. Blass must have been unpleasant, surely?"

Ron had taken out a tissue and was wiping his face. He half-closed his eyes. But he smiled. "It's over now," he said.

"And how relieved we all are!" Dr. Barth said. "The committee really should apologize, Ron, and also thank Dean Harr for helping us out with a matter that shouldn't have taken up his valuable time—only a minor departmental issue—"

"Just a minute," Mason said. "Wait. Just a minute. I . . . I don't understand. Were the *yeses* and the *no's* reversed? Wait, I . . . I might have gotten the instructions wrong. . . ."

"You didn't get them wrong," Dr. May said, with a bright, malicious smile.

"But I don't understand. . . . I just don't understand," Mason said. He stared at them all. That day, he had even put on a light yellow shirt, sporty and spring-like; but now he looked aged. "I thought . . . an issue like this . . . plagiarism . . . the standards of our profession . . . I thought . . . I. . . . What does this mean? What happened?"

"*Plagiarism* is a legal term," Dr. Barth said. "It must be used very, very carefully, I believe . . . for if accused of plagiarism, a man might sue for slander, you know. Under our law. Is that correct, Dean Harr?"

"Yes, and very odd it is!—that a man might even have grounds for a suit though the plagiarism be proved. . . . The law is very odd, isn't it?" Dean Harr said cheerfully. He had stood and was now rubbing his hands together, energetically. "But I don't suppose you know much about law, Dr. Mason . . . ?"

"Just a minute, this hearing can't be dismissed," Mason said angrily. "Something went on here! I—I know that something went on—"

"—and plagiarism, if one must use so crude a term," Dr. Barth said, "is perhaps not provable anyway? Never provable, I should say."

"Never," Dr. Snyder said grimly.

"Never," said Dr. May. And, with a grudging sideways acknowledgement of Dr. Thayer, he said, "In any case Robinson here quite dramatically demonstrated . . . at our first meeting . . . how the completely-informed scholar may lightly trip back through the maze of the tradition . . . eh? And trace everything back to primary sources, no doubt even to a primary source if necessary. It was remarkably illuminating. . . . But the correct Shakespeare is, I believe, 'Nothing will come *of* nothing.' You misquoted the line as *from* nothing, I believe."

Thayer laughed angrily.

". . . but wait, wait," Mason said, seeing they were about to stand. "This is all beside the point. You're all confusing me. I *know* something went on here—"

"*Nothing plagiarizes nothing*," Thayer said suddenly.

"Ah, is that also a quotation?" Dr. May asked. "It isn't original with you, is it, Robinson? It couldn't be—original with you, could it?"

"*Life plagiarizes life*," Thayer said.

Now they were really about to stand and Mason jumped to his feet to protest. "Wait. Please. *Wait*. How did this come about—this reversal? Has that ugly pack of Blass students threatened the university? Are they putting pressure on you? Is he blackmailing you somehow? I just cannot believe—"

"Heva, did you notice what Dr. Thayer just said? A very original remark, evidently—*Life plagiarizes life*. We'll all remember that," Dr. May said.

"—no, wait," Mason said. "What about the department's standards?—our respect for scholarship? What has come over you? If the senior staff, of all people, don't maintain standards—if—Why, it will usher in a new era of barbarism, of anarchy! I'll take this issue to the whole department, if you people refuse to act responsibly—it is an ethical imperative of ours—I'll insist upon a meeting of the entire department and—"

"I wouldn't do that if I were you," Dr. Barth said mildly.

"What?"

"I wouldn't do that,' Dr. Barth said.

"No," Dean Harr said slowly, emphasizing each word, "I wouldn't do that."

Mason looked from face to face. He was very pale. "Is that a—?" he said, his voice breaking, and said again, "Is that a threat? A threat? Is that a threat against *me*? Am I being threatened now? *I*? Is my position being threatened? When all I did was—I tried to maintain—I—I labored for weeks to present case—my ethical responsibilities—"

No one spoke. Dr. May lit his pipe. Mason said, "But I won't be intimidated. I won't. I won't be intimidated. I'll expose you all. I'll resign. Keep your fifth-rate plagiarist poet, hide him and encourage him and what he represents, cast me out, go ahead and cast *me* out, I'll expose all of you—you'll regret this day—I'll get justice—"

But he never did: he had some sort of breakdown, returned to Oakville to live with his parents, and people at Hilberry gradually forgot about him.

THE BIRTH OF TRAGEDY

for G. B.

W hat are we going to do? All of us—*all* of us? What do you think will happen? What are *you* going to do, Barry?"

The girl, with her plain stark remorseless face, was staring at him as if she thought him an ally. But he hadn't given up yet. He was not going to give up at all. So he said, cautiously, apologetically: "I have one more university to hear from."

"*You* do?"

"Yes, one more to hear from," he said, blushing.

He was completing his senior year at the University of Michigan; he was twenty-two years old, a shy, long-haired, impoverished young man, who never asked his friends the questions now asked him, the same questions his mother asked in her letters: *What are you going to do next year? Can you get a job? Can you get money from a graduate school somewhere?—anywhere? What will happen to you? Are you going to apply for welfare . . . ?*

"What is it?" the girl asked.

"Just a teaching assistantship, just enough money to get me through," he mumbled, uneasily, "it's only a small college in Canada and . . . and they haven't turned me down yet. . . . I got a form letter a month ago saying my application was still being considered, so . . . so . . . so I haven't given up yet," he said. The girl, an honors physics major with a very high average, had had one interview for a job, only one: that had been a few weeks ago and she'd heard nothing since. She had dropped out of her classes and slept

105

fourteen hours a day at times, and at other times evidently didn't sleep at all but called up people she knew, daytime or nighttime, to talk breathlessly and maniacally about the "future." She met Barry on the street or in the library and cornered him, asking if he'd heard about a mutual friend who evidently had a job—a teaching job in Fairbanks, Alaska—at least that was the rumor—did Barry know if it was true?—and asking him if he'd heard the terrible news, that a girl had evidently thrown herself out of the window of her dormitory room, had fallen eight floors to the pavement and had died—had he heard who she was, and why she'd done it?

Barry began to stay awake most of the night, smoking. He thought of the small, near-unknown college in Ontario, near the Lake. *If only. . . . If. . . .* He smoked cigarettes though he couldn't afford them and really despised people who smoked, he picked at his teeth, at his fingernails, at his toenails, waiting and wondering, and never in his life was he to experience such agony again: *After the first death there is no other*, he told himself wryly. He had done his senior honors thesis on the poetry of Dylan Thomas, which he loved. He wanted to teach poetry like that: he had decided, only this past year, that he wanted to be a teacher. His first three years in Ann Arbor he'd been skeptical, prematurely suspicious of life, and he had managed to get through most of his courses with fairly good grades, though he had not worked hard. His I. Q. was supposed to be quite high, so his mother had told him, and he had relied on it to get him through. . . . he rather regretted that, now; he had decided that he was a serious young man after all. And the others were serious too, suddenly: even bitter ironic Mady, who telephoned him too often now and began even to speak of the future in terms of "us," "people like us," "you and me. . . ." She had nothing to look to, she complained, *not even marriage.*

Thank God, Hilberry College accepted him.

He had travelled through Western Ontario a few times, on his way to visit friends of his in Toronto who had moved there to avoid the draft, but he'd never gone out of his way to visit Hilberry College. When he arrived there, the first week in September, he was prepared to love it—and only a little disappointed in its small, contained campus, its mismatched but unpretentious architecture, and the unexciting, amiable, middle-aged men who constituted the graduate faculty. The department boasted one poet—a short, gregarious man named Blass—and one rather flamboyantly-dressed black man in his thirties, but neither of these men taught graduate seminars. What was worse, Barry had evidently been picked by a professor named Thayer, Robinson Thayer, to assist him with a large lecture-course in Shakespeare—Thayer was the department's outstanding scholar, the author of a study of Shakespeare's legal imagery that was evidently considered an important work, though Barry had never heard of it. Dr. Thayer was in his early fifties but looked older: he had a bemused, sallow, heavily-creased face, iron-gray hair that was kept trimmed so short that his scalp sometimes showed through, and he had only three suits which he wore in rotation and which Barry came to know well. Two were gray and the other was a very dark color, which sometimes appeared to be brown and at other times green. Barry was so grateful to be enrolled in the graduate program at Hilberry that he was prepared to love even Dr. Thayer, unfriendly and unfashionable as Thayer appeared. He was in sharp contrast to the man who'd taught Barry Shakespeare at Ann Arbor, a youthful, handsome, melodramatic professor who left the podium frequently to act out important scenes for the class —mad scenes and love scenes were his specialty.

But Hilberry College was not the University of Michigan. And Barry was not the old Barry, either. Having come so close to being rejected by the world, having learned a quite serious humility, he had his long hair cut so that it only curled down around his collar, he wore shoes and socks and, for his conferences with Dr. Thayer, even a freshly-laundered shirt. He shaved on Tuesdays and Thursdays, when he attended Dr. Thayer's lectures, sitting attentively at the very back of the hall and taking notes all period long. As Thayer's teaching assistant it would be Barry's job to take attendance, help grade quizzes and exams, and occasionally, if Thayer asked him, to take over the class.

Thayer was doubtful about letting Barry teach, however. At their first conference—held in Thayer's office in the Humanities Building—he stared at Barry for some time without speaking, the creases around his mouth settled into place as if he might sit there, like that, forever. He was wearing one of the gray suits, an old-fashioned pin-striped suit with sleeves that were slightly too long. He said, shaking his head philosophically: "*You* want to teach in college? *You*? . . . But I suppose you have your reasons. I suppose you have immense confidence in yourself."

Barry looked at the man sadly. He did not know what to say, so he sat there, trying to smile, in a straight-back chair pulled up close to Dr. Thayer's big desk. Behind the desk Thayer leaned back in a brown leather wing-back chair, smiling mysteriously. He appeared to be waiting for Barry to speak, so Barry began to say that he would be content just to correct papers and take attendance and do any other tasks Dr. Thayer required of him—he hoped someday to teach, yes, but he didn't dare hope—and anyway he was terrified of— But Thayer interrupted him almost at once.

"Don't pretend to be humble," he laughed. "I know the way you students talk when you're alone—in the men's room, for instance, I hear remarkable things. I doubt that I will call upon your teaching abilities until much later in the year, Mr. Sommers, if at all, but I do insist that my teaching assistants attend all of my lectures and that they do a little extra clerical work for me—I'm writing an article on a contemporary of Shakespeare's named Sturgess, whom I suppose you've never heard of?—no?—and I need a little research done for me, and I'd like you also to watch carefully during our class to see who is taking notes and who isn't; I have my reasons for wanting special information about my students. After all, if they can send spies to watch me I can certainly use spies to watch them."

"Spies?" Barry asked.

"Yes, the student newspaper runs exposé articles now and then, and no one is safe, but I've lived with that sort of thing for years now," Thayer said, almost merrily, "and they've never found me unprepared for a lecture yet. Never. It's an exciting life, in its own way! ... You know, Mr. Sommers, we may learn to get along well, you and I. You seem a fairly decent young man. You seem to have actually washed and shaved and though you're wearing jeans—those are jeans, aren't they?—at least you're not wearing bib overalls and parachute boots, like the teaching assistant the department tried to force on me last year. In fact," he said, suddenly smiling, "in fact it may work out well. I won't anticipate any trouble. And I suggest you don't either, if you please."

"No, sir. I won't. I certainly won't," Barry said.

"Well, welcome to Hilberry and to our graduate program in English. We're not Ann Arbor but then neither is Ann Arbor Oxford, eh?"

Dr. Thayer had received his advance degrees at University College, Oxford. His lectures were delivered in a rapid monotone, punctuated by pauses in which he looked up from his notes, sometimes pointedly, dramatically, as if expecting response of some kind from the students—though they were usually bent over their notebooks, writing or doodling, or staring toward the windows, day-dreaming; and sometimes, confronted with such evident stupidity, he smiled sardonically and said something about the difference in quality between Canadian and American students on the one hand and English students on the other. He contrasted Hilberry with Oxford. Then, as if deliberately forcing himself to back down, *as if making a show of backing down*, he muttered that of course times have changed, the world had changed, and this college was as good a college as one might find in southern Ontario.

Barry came to admire the man, in a way. He feared and disliked him, but had to acknowledge that he really knew everything about Shakespeare—everything that was historical, at least—and his reading of the famous passages was only a little forced, a little pompous. Barry even began to get angry when some of the students turned to grin at each other, during Thayer's lectures; and when Thayer lost his temper and ordered a hulking young man out of the room—crying "Leave! Please leave! Simply take the nearest exit and leave!"—Barry's heart pounded with indignation. He knew

Thayer was making a mistake, but somehow he approved and was glad Thayer had kicked that bastard out.

When students came to Barry's cubicle, in the teaching assistants' big common office, he was sympathetic with their complaints but never sided with them against Dr. Thayer. Thayer went over the tests Barry had graded, careful to mark spelling errors and to question points Barry had accepted, and he often crossed out Barry's grades and substituted lower grades; but Barry usually agreed with his corrections. When Blass, the department poet, hung around the graduate students' office and gossiped, amazing them with anecdotes about Dr. Thayer, Barry sat frowning, not joining in the laughter. Blass told them of how Dr. Thayer had turned up drunk and disheveled at a conference in Toronto, in order to challenge a Renaissance scholar who was delivering a paper on some minor playwright—Sturgess, the name was, though no one had ever heard of him—and it had even gotten in the local newspaper. That had happened seven or eight years ago. "Since then he's been crafty and quiet," Blass said, "and he evidently stopped drinking. He must have stopped drinking. . . . Have you ever smelled liquor on his breath, Barry?—you're the only one he allows close enough to him to judge—"

Barry said irritably that he had never smelled liquor on Thayer's breath. And he didn't believe that story, either.

"But it's true! And there are even secret details to it that only the chairman of the department and the dean know," Blass said. "The man is an utter mystery. . . . I've figured out everyone here except him. I can't quite figure him out. You know he despises the drama students?—if he kicks anyone out of class it's always a drama student, because he has a feud of some kind going with the chairman of the drama department. But only a few years ago they got along very well—Dr. Thayer, believe it or not, acted in a play the drama department put on—he was Iago, believe it or not! And he was really good, in spite of his age. In fact he was incredibly good. They had him made up to look twenty years younger, and he *did* look young, and his voice and even the way he paced around on stage were so believable—you really believed, you really understood the play. You understood why it had to happen the way it did. Then Thayer got temperamental, or there was a disagreement of some kind, and he walked out one night just before curtain-time— and everybody was furious with him. Even the president of the university tried to talk him into going back. But no, he wouldn't listen. . . . And another thing happened just last April: he was involved in a disagreement of some kind with his landlord, and moved out to the Holiday Inn, just hired a van and moved out one morning. He broke his lease and his landlord tried to sue him, and it got in the papers, and a sister of his—or an aunt—showed up, from Calgary, a husky old gal as tough as Thayer himself. She looked just like him, her hair was even cropped off short, and she wore a herringbone pants-suit. . . . She was around here for a few weeks, even went to his lectures and hung around his office, and nobody knew what she wanted, though she told one of the secretaries that she was a registered psychotherapist. Thayer seemed to avoid her. I guess he's still living at the Holiday Inn. Or is he living somewhere else now, Barry?"

"Why do you ask me?" Barry said. "I don't know anything about him."

"You know more than the rest of us," Blass said.

As if Thayer sensed how Barry defended him, he began to invite Barry into his office after class. He would close the door and offer Barry a glass of sherry—which Barry usually declined—and sit in his leather chair, swivelling to one side in order to stare out the window at the slate-gray Ontario sky, as if wondering what to say to his young guest. One day in late November he cleared his throat and said, hesitantly, "You really can let your hair grow back if you like. I saw your photograph on your application, you know— I saw how you looked before. In fact, I sorted through the graduate applications—I'm head of the graduate committee, as you may know—and I didn't at all mind your original appearance. In fact it was rather striking—it was Elizabethan."

111

Barry was too surprised to reply. But Thayer rattled on, not looking at him, as if eager to change the subject. He asked Barry how it might be that while attendance in his class was so low, students managed to answer most of the questions on his exams—did Barry think they took turns coming to class, and then shared the notes? Did he think there were master-notes somewhere on campus, compiled from previous years and mimeographed and sold? *Had Barry ever come across those notes?* Barry had not. Thayer did not reply for a while. He was turning a bronze letter-opener in his fingers; it had a lion's head, the teeth and tongue exaggerated. Barry saw a trickle of perspiration run down Thayer's face, from his left temple all the way down to his jaw.

He wanted to leave, but did not dare move.

Thayer poured a glass of sherry for himself, drank it down, and poured another. He glanced at Barry. ". . . it's certainly a fine opportunity for all of us . . . senior faculty and younger people . . . yes, indeed . . . I don't at all mind working closely with the up-and-coming . . . after all, you do represent the future. And you're much nicer than that savage in the overalls. . . . He was dropped from our program in mid-year, he simply didn't work out as an assistant to me, it truly puzzled me how the administration expected me to work with such a creature. The departmental head—I'm telling you this in confidence, Barry—tried to reinstate the boy, actually tried to argue with me over him, and I suspect—though I never made my suspicions public—that Dr. Barth was being bribed by the boy's parents. It's a very complex, sinister world here—but of course exhilarating, if you don't weaken. It's like a Shakespearean play—without the fifth act. The fourth act just goes on and on, scenes of high tragedy alternate with scenes of the most contemptible, gross comedy—but I enjoy it all, really. You will too, Barry, when you arrive at my age.—What are you staring at?"

"Staring at? Nothing—"

"You seemed to be staring at me."

"I wasn't. I didn't mean to."

". . . this letter-opener was given to me by Dr. Mittelstaedt, do you know him? He runs the Drama Department. He gave me this

112

knife as a token of his buried esteem, his peculiar warped admiration for me . . . he's under the illusion, as many members of our faculty are, that I am a man of certain violent impulses. Therefore the knife. Therefore a kind of hint, a dramatic hint. This world, Barry," Thayer said suddenly, almost passionately, leaning forward to gesture across his wide, clean, smooth-polished desk, "this world is all *drama*. As long as you know that and realize that other people are feverishly writing scenarios in order to trap you in them, you'll survive. Otherwise I can't encourage you. Do you understand?"

Barry did not understand. He was staring at the bronze letteropener, wondering what had brought him here, to this office, to Dr. Thayer's late-afternoon book-shelved office, to the sweet odor of sherry and the coy glinting of a weapon. The door was closed to the corridor. Barry had the strange idea that someone was out there, however, having approached Thayer's office to knock at the door . . . now just standing there, listening.

"The complex chain of circumstances that brought you here, to this very place, this afternoon," Thayer said, as if reading Barry's mind, "is not nearly so mysterious to the person who wrote the scenario, as it may be to you. Consider: a man leafing through a stack of applications for our Master's Degree program, a little bored, perhaps a little jaded . . . and a few faces striking enough to force him to pause. Only a few. Out of a mountain of photographs one will find himself pausing only over a very few. . . . Do you have to be somewhere, Barry? You appear to be anxious to leave?"

Barry said no, he wasn't anxious to leave, but he had to leave . . . he had to get to the . . . .

". . . to the library, or the bookstore, or a class, yes, yes," Thayer said quickly, as if completing a line of dialogue for him "I understand. *Summer's lease hath all too short a date.*" He finished the glass of sherry and hesitated, as if not wanting to set the glass down for fear that gesture might release Barry. "I really wanted to talk to you about a matter of professional importance, about your teaching apprenticeship. I'd like you to give your first lecture on

Tuesday morning."

"*Tuesday* morning?"

"Yes, Tuesday morning. You realize that your scholarship obliges you to perform certain teaching duties, don't you?—or did you imagine it was nothing but sitting at the rear of the lecture-hall, day-dreaming and pretending to take notes in order to flatter me?—I'm not that egotistical, after all! Though occasionally you do cut my lecture, I believe you were absent last Tuesday, weren't you?"

Barry tried to explain that he'd had an attack of the flu—

"No, no, don't apologize," Thayer said quickly, "*nor think the bitterness of absence sour. . . .*" with a wave of his hand, to show he was not offended; yet somehow offended. "But I am most interested in observing your first lecture, since your stated desire to enter the teaching profession . . . on your application, I believe, you wrote *university professor* . . . your desire brings us to certain blunt pragmatic matters of measurement. I am required to judge your capacity for continuing in our program, as you probably know, beyond the Master's level and into the more advanced program. . . . You did indicate that you wanted a Doctorate of Philosophy? . . . in 'English Literature'?"

"Yes," Barry said. "But I didn't think . . . I wasn't prepared to. . . ."

"I know, I know, you're very modest," Thayer said, getting to his feet. He set the glass down; he rubbed his hands together as if the interview were concluded. Barry got slowly to his feet. "But your transcript from the University of Michigan indicates a fairly high degree of achievement . . . not nearly as high as most of our graduate students, of course, but *they* seem like rather crude predictable fellows, and you're quite different, as you must realize. We'll see."

Barry realized that he was supposed to leave. He stared at Thayer. For the first time, he realized that the man was taller than he: that his face was shrewd, prim, amused, and somehow malleable. Barry felt, dizzily, that the flesh of that face could suddenly shift into any shape, any set of features. ". . . but what should I do? What should my lecture be about? I. . . ."

"Don't be modest! Deliver your first public lecture on a challenging subject: on the mysterious 'double-time' plots of *Othello* and *Troilus and Cressida*. Or, better yet, Shakespeare's borrowings from Sturgess, with an emphasis upon *King Lear*."

Barry was nodding, vaguely. Thayer sighed as if releasing him, as if preparing for another task—simply waiting for his guest to leave. But Barry stood there.

"You've read *King Lear*, haven't you?"

"Oh yes, yes. I've read *King Lear*. . . ."

Thayer went to the door and opened it, slowly, with a gracious, self-conscious manner as if he realized he might be rude, in nearly telling his guest to leave; yet he had to open the door, after all. Otherwise his guest would never leave. Barry looked wildly out into the corridor, not knowing why he looked—no one was there— he stared helplessly all the way down to the far end, where a cleaning lady was pushing a cart. A broom stuck out of the cart. "Is something wrong? You seem rather edgy," Thayer said.

"It must be the flu, the aftermath of the flu," Barry said.

"Yes, you look a little pale; you look undernourished."

Barry gathered his things—picked up his green canvas book-bag —and turned to leave. He passed quite close to Dr. Thayer, who moved back, almost imperceptibly. As he was walking away, walking toward the cleaning lady, he heard Thayer make a sound with his mouth as if he'd just realized something—a kind of sharp *tsking*-sound—and Barry looked around hopefully. Thayer was hurrying after him. "I just thought of something, only this moment —you'd probably appreciate a little help with the lecture? I mean, of course, just some minimal help? . . . Since it's such an important event in your career . . . ?"

"Yes, Dr. Thayer," Barry said quickly.

". . . and even with your swift intelligence and admirable background, you probably wouldn't be insulted if I coached you a little? . . . Let's say on Monday evening, if that's convenient for you? Monday evening of next week? Is that convenient for you, Barry?"

"Yes, thank God," Barry said, "I mean yes. It's very convenient—"

Dr. Thayer no longer lived at the Holiday Inn, but rented, week by week, a room with an efficiency kitchen at the Rest-a-While Motel, a one-story concrete structure, painted green, facing the broad, noisy highway that led east to Niagara Falls and west to Hamilton. A pink neon sign with some of its tubing unlit announced the motel, which Barry found after some difficulty. Dr. Thayer had given him the correct number, but the motel was evidently in a zone that had had its street numbers changed recently, because two numbers—both in the thousands—were nailed onto the wooden frame of the office door. So Barry was a few minutes late when he knocked at the door to Room 11. He was out of breath from having trudged up and down the highway and had gotten panicked, knowing how Dr. Thayer would be furious if he were late.

But when Thayer opened the door he seemed genuinely pleased to see Barry: he smiled warmly and shook his hand and invited him in. "It isn't much, but . . . but I've grown to think of it as home," he said. The motel room was drably furnished, but Thayer had brightened it up with a vase of flowers—fresh roses—set atop the television set. The set was not turned on. The bedspread was a shiny, satiny quilt with aqua and rust sunburst designs in it, and a number of small satin-covered pillows, of various colors, had been strewn across the bed and placed on the room's two vinyl-covered chairs. Barry, out of breath, his shoulder aching from the weight of the book-bag he'd been carrying for the past hour, sat in the nearer of the chairs. Dr. Thayer chattered about the noise from the traffic and the occasional noises from other rooms and how healthy and fresh-faced Barry was from his walk, and would he like a drink?—he'd just fixed himself a Scotch on the rocks and had started dinner, he hoped Barry wasn't too hungry, he was very slow and fastidious about preparing important meals. Barry accepted the Scotch without exactly agreeing to have it. He was surprised at Dr. Thayer's exuberance and his generous, unforced conversation; Thayer was even wearing an outfit Barry had never seen

116

before, a monogrammed lemon-green shirt and navy blue trousers cut trimly at the knee and flaring out at the ankle, and calfskin boots with square, raised heels.

"A drink?—ah, I've already made you one!" Thayer said cheerfully. "Now just relax while I check a little something that's simmering on the stove—our first course—can you smell it?—that's *Trifolgi con Cotechini e Lenticchie*, how's that for a melodious sound! I've been very pleased and excited all day, at the way life is working itself out— Would you like some more ice, Barry? Or is your drink suitable?"

"It's fine," Barry said. He had set the big, thick-cut glass down on the rug. He wondered if he should get his notebook out of his book-bag, but Thayer probably wasn't ready yet to talk about the next day's lecture. He kept darting in and out of the little alcove where the kitchen was, murmuring to himself *Now I must watch the time,* then glancing over at Barry and smiling, in embarrassment.

"You're the first dinner guest I've had in some time," he confessed. He sat in the other chair, pulling it closer to Barry. "Now, let's see, your lecture for tomorrow, you're probably still concerned about that . . . we're beginning *Hamlet,* aren't we? I believe that's on the syllabus."

"*Hamlet?*" said Barry. "I thought I was supposed to talk about Shakespeare and Sturgess."

"Ah, Shakespeare and Sturgess!" Dr. Thayer nodded. He sipped at his drink, rattling the ice cubes; his face looked heated, perhaps from the stove, and he kept smiling at Barry in an encouraging, patient manner. "My favorite topic—how a man of genius was abused, his unpublished work ransacked, in order that another, more politically-minded, more *diabolical* personality should come to be immortal. . . . Not," he said hastily, "that Shakespeare himself wasn't a genius. He was. I admire Shakespeare very much. His command of language!—yes, all that, all that sort of thing—if you care for that sort of thing— Well, are you excited about tomorrow morning? Just think, Barry, tomorrow at eleven your career officially begins!"

117

"Dr. Thayer, I'm a little concerned about—"

"You and your modesty! Why, your generation is always trying to put the rest of us off-balance, feigning such humility," Dr. Thayer teased. He looked youthful, exuberant. Barry, who had been working in the university library for most of the day, felt quite tired. "Nothing to worry about, not a thing—would you like your drink freshened?—why, you haven't touched it!—Barry, please don't worry, I have all the notes for your lecture in my filing cabinet at school—all you'll need, and more—in fact I have a hundred-page unpublished manuscript, on the relationship between Shakespeare and Sturgess. *Please* don't worry!"

He went back into the alcove, humming. Barry, who had not eaten since noon, and who'd then eaten only a quick lunch at the student union, wondered how he would get through this evening. There was something so bright and hectic and rushed about Thayer. . . . And the lecture-notes were at the university, not here! He was very confused. When Thayer returned, still humming, Barry tried to explain that he had searched through a number of scholarly books and periodicals, but had only discovered three articles on the Shakespeare-Sturgess relationship, two of them by Dr. Thayer himself and the third by a man named—

"Oh, that idiot," Thayer snorted. He waved his hand in Barry's face. "Please don't spoil our evening. As I said, this is the first entertaining I've dared in some time . . . I once lived in an apartment with a quite handsome kitchen, a stove with four large burners . . . an excellent refrigerator and freezing unit . . . even a garbage disposal. . . . But here I am, ejected from my former life, but quite cheerful as you can see! . . . You'll discover a secret about me tonight, Barry, that nobody knows at the university. . . . I'm really a romantic. A very romantic, sentimental individual . . . secretly, I've been taking lessons in Italian cuisine, at a cooking school in Hamilton. My class meets every Saturday morning. I think you'll be pleased with the results. . . . No, don't you dare! You leave that awful book-bag of yours alone! This is an evening to celebrate, Barry, and not to soil with academic considerations. I thought we'd have a celebration tonight, Barry . . . I ran all over town getting the right wine for us. I have to take a taxi everywhere, as I may have mentioned; I no longer drive. But I located a truly excellent wine, I think you'll approve of it, now don't look so harrassed and pale! You're probably just hungry."

"Actually, I'm a little worried about tomorrow morning," Barry said carefully. "There are a hundred and fifteen students in your course . . . and they're so sophisticated . . . and demanding . . . I'm getting a litle worried, well frankly *very* worried, about how I'll do. . . . I only have about ten minutes' worth of a lecture so far. . . ."

Dr. Thayer waved this away, chuckling. He got to his feet again and went back to the stove. Barry looked sadly around the room; on a night-table beside the bed, a small travelling clock in an alligator-skin case read 9:30. It was already 9:30 Monday evening, and he had to give his lecture the next morning at 11. He wished that Dr. Thayer would quiet down. But in the little six-by-nine kitchen he was humming and whistling happily through his teeth. He leaned around to look at Barry and said, "These professor-student assignments are very valuable, aren't they?—it allows for a kind of working apprenticeship, and of course the professor is like a big brother, able to watch and guide and perhaps even learn a bit. We're never too old to learn, of course. . . . It isn't known in the department, is it, that I'm a gourmet cook? I know they whisper ugly, absurd, totally incredible stories about me, but I have never overheard anyone gossiping about my trips to Hamilton. . . . Have you?"

"No, never," Barry said nervously.

Thayer brought the bottle of Scotch back, and poured more into Barry's glass. Now it was filled right to the brim. He dragged a small coffee table over and began to set two places, chattering excitedly. There was a ripe, nutty, sweet odor about him; Barry realized that he was getting drunk. From time to time he would forget what he was talking about and recite lines from Shakespeare, from the sonnets—"*Weary with toil, I haste me to my bed . . . but then begins, ah yes begins, begins a journey in my head . . . for then my thoughts, from far where I abide . . . intend a zealous pil-*

grimage to thee . . . Yes, that's very nice, very apt. Very well-worded. And all *his*, Shakespeare's own words!—you must acknowledge Shakespeare where he is supremely himself and not plagiarizing from others. He has a true gift for language. . . . Ah, how does it go. . . .

> A woman's face, with Nature's own hand painted,
> Hast thou, the master-mistress of my passion;
> A woman's gentle heart, but not acquainted
> With shifting change, as is false women's fashion;
> An eye more bright than theirs, less false in rolling,
> Gilding the object whereupon it gazeth;
> A man in hue all hues in his controlling,
> Which steals men's eyes and women's souls amazeth.
> And for a woman wert thou first created,
> Till Nature as she wrought thee fell a-doting,
> And by addition me of thee defeated
> By adding one thing to my purpose nothing.
> > But since she pricked thee out for women's pleasure,
> > Mine be thy love, and thy love's use their treasure.

That too is his own invention—all but line four, the *shifting change* imagery. That, of course, is Sturgess—but what do we care for Sturgess tonight? Or for anyone? Why, Barry, what is wrong?"

Barry had been staring into space, as if a sudden illumination were flaring inside him, rich and raw as pain. He was breathing shallowly, through his mouth.

"Barry—?"

Barry got to his feet. He stopped to grab his book-bag. "Dr. Thayer, I think I'd better leave now—"

"What? Leave? *Now?*"

"Yes, I think—I think—I think I'd better leave now—"

"What!"

Barry did not dare to look at the man. Thayer was standing there, blocking his way; he held clutched in one hand a white linen napkin and a soup spoon, an antique silver spoon that was slightly tarnished. He swayed, drunkenly. He said, "My boy, really . . . you

don't dare . . . after I spent eighteen dollars on taxi fares alone . . .
not to mention the excitement, the strain on my nerves . . . and the
red mullet! . . . how it stank up everything, the smell is on my good
gray suit! . . . oh no, no you don't, no, not after the red mullet and
the barbarian who tried to sell me red snapper instead! . . . we're
going to feast on *Ziti con Triglie ed Uova*, no you don't, give me
that disgusting smelly book-bag, you're teasing me, you're testing
me . . . to see if I'll alter when I alteration find or bend with, eh,
bend with the remover to remove . . . isn't that it? That must be
your strategy! Otherwise why are you here? *Just why are you
here?*"

He was beginning to shout. Barry got away from him, knocking
against the little coffee table and sending the things flying, saying,
"Dr. Thayer, please, Dr. Thayer let me out, Dr. Thayer, my God,
oh please let me out," but Thayer heard none of this and was half-
sobbing, about Barry having no right, no rights, who did he think
he was?—he didn't even exist yet!— He had deliberately flaunted
himself two years ago, Thayer cried, did he dare deny it?—
shameless, absolutely shameless!—and Mittelstaedt knew everything about it and would confirm the cruel arrogance and shame-
lessness of that behavior, though Mittelstaedt was an enemy now—
yet he would side with Robinson Thayer against a little tramp like
him. Barry tried to explain that he was new here at Hilberry, he'd
only arrived three months ago, but Thayer heard nothing, now
tearing at the collar of his green shirt, furiously, following Barry
as he backed to the door, crying into his face that this was in total
violation of the evening's scenario, that Barry was a vicious per-
verted little schemer who would pay dearly, with his life's blood,
for this fantastic crime—Barry grabbed the doorknob and yanked
the door open, almost sobbing himself, he was so frightened, trying
to apologize in a voice he'd never heard before *My God, no, I'm
sorry, let me go, no*—but Thayer interrupted him, his voice breaking, breaking downward into a quieter, saner key: "I saw you joking
around in the Common Room with that twit, the poet what's-his-
name, and that disgusting nigger with the goatee and the sideburns
and the fancy ascots—how *could* you! I should have known then,

121

it makes me absolutely ill to think of my folly, you a crude barbaric creature who never deserved your face and your curly hair—it's my tragedy always to stoop too low—my tragedy always, always, to be excluded! —You look so innocent in that fake stagy terror, but you'll regret this, my God how you will regret this—"

"Dr. Thayer, the lecture—"

"Why am I always cheated, always excluded from life! That idiot Mittelstaedt has a perfectly idyllic relationship with *his* teaching assistant, and even that nigger, even *he*!—has a big floppy floozy bleached-blond chum he goes swimming with—This university exists only to degrade me! They plot and joke about my scholarship, my trips to Hamilton, my sister's mad scheme to have me committed, my adviser at Oxford, who was so viciously clubbed to death in Soho and his reputation absolutely ruined by the *TLS*—oh, the vicious things!—and now you've taken your place among them, among my enemies—"

Barry had backed out of the room, clutching his book-bag to his chest. "Dr. Thayer, no, I—I came here for—to learn to—to be a teacher—to get in the Ph.D. program and—and—"

"*What* Ph.D. program, you little idiot?" Thayer laughed. "We're dropping it after this year—the province of Ontario is shutting us down—it was all a ruse, my boy, we need students and you show up, perfectly idiotic little boys and girls who can't spell, who know no Latin and less Greek, many of you from the States—Go back! Leave! Get out of here! Out of my motel room! *Out, out! Leave!*"

*　　*　　*　　*

Barry ran much of the way back to his room, and there, after having stood for a long space of time, in the center of his room, still, paralyzed, not even thinking of what had happened, he decided he would go through with the lecture: he would write up a lecture and deliver it. Maybe that was what he should do. Maybe Thayer would change his mind. Maybe. . . . Maybe Thayer would not remember. He had been drunk, he had been so drunk his face turned

122

sickly-pale, like dough. . . . *You'll regret this*, he had said, but maybe he would not remember.

So Barry stayed up all night, trying to splice together notes for a lecture. For a while he worked quickly, almost euphorically, scribbling information about the complicated history of the First Folio and the mysterious absence of records of Shakespeare's whereabouts during certain crucial years; then, glancing back through his notes, Barry saw how thin they were, how disorganized and pointless, and—it was now after four in the morning—he began to feel real panic, and, his throat suddenly dry, he pawed frantically through reference books he'd brought home from the library —huge, 1000-page books with dusty covers and loose bindings— and his mind raced with he horror of it all, now it was nearly five o'clock and he had only six hours left—and then as he jotted down a new set of notes taken from a history of Holinshed's *Chronicles* he had the eerie feeling he'd done this before, he'd jotted all these notes down before—he shoved the book aside, and opened another large book, this one called *Will Shake-Speare's Handwriting in "The Booke of Sir Thomas Moore"*—evidently there was an Elizabethan manuscript by that title in six different handwritings— and dizzily, helplessly, once again Barry had the feeling he'd done all this before.

He leafed through the notes he'd taken in Thayer's lectures— and there it all was. Evidently Thayer had simply transcribed notes from these old books and read them off, lecture after lecture . . . it was all historical information . . . all facts and "hotly-contested" claims of authorship. . . . For a while Barry was depressed by this discovery. Then, feebly, he thought it was probably a good thing, he should feel encouraged. . . . If Dr. Thayer had done it, he too could do it. Perhaps that was all he needed to do: copy notes from library books.

So he spent the rest of the time copying notes. His fingers turned cold with a growing terror of the lecture itself, the hideous thought of the students actually trooping into the lecture-room . . . but he forced the thought out of his mind and continued writing, frantically, beginning to abbreviate words since time was running out. . . .

He had enough information to get him through the class-period, he believed, if he spoke slowly enough. He must remember to speak slowly. . . . But he felt so strange, so light-headed, that when the actual thought of the lecture-room rose in his mind he went cold with terror, knowing that he would never get through it and that his life was over.

He took notes until the last minute, then hurried over to the campus, and it amazed him—how people were strolling around, so calmly, so casually! Some of them were even talking together and smiling. He had decided to bring along with him the most valuable of the books, *The Editorial Problem in Shakespeare*, and had certain pages marked with tiny green slips of paper, in case he should run out of lecture notes. . . . He could always read to them, as Thayer often did. Almost, going up the stairs to the second floor of the Humanities Building, being crowded and jostled by the students thundering their way up past him, almost, holding the heavy book, he began to think that he would succeed.

But as soon as he entered the lecture-hall he felt panic. He had never realized how big this room was. My God, he thought, staring out at the rows of seats, at the students already beginning to settle in their desks and arrange their long legs in the aisles, my God, how can this be?—he walked slowly into the room, up to the lectern at the front of the room, as if in a trance of horror, everything in him light and weightless and yet tinged with a shrewd greenish-black nausea. *He was going to be sick.* He saw how they stared at him, surprised. Dr. Thayer had forgotten to announce that Barry was going to take over the class today. . . . Barry let his books and notes fall onto the lectern, as if losing his strength suddenly. He stared at one of the tiny green slips that had fallen out of its place. Something about red mullet, something about odors. He felt sick: he was going to be sick. He did not dare glance up at the students, now settling in, settling down, with a peculiar sharp expectancy new to this class. They realized he would be sick and were waiting. They could see the nausea squirming in him, they could see how ghastly-pale his face was . . . like unbaked dough . . . they were waiting keenly, delightedly, waiting to see him vomit. . . .

Barry had no watch and he was so dazed he nearly forgot to check the time, on a big wall clock behind him. It was after eleven! A half-dozen more students crowded in through the door, and behind them Dr. Thayer himself, who did no more than glance at Barry. He was carrying some sort of machine. A tape-recorder? He looked exactly as he always looked, maybe a little more sallow, but he wore the better of his gray suits and his hair was perfectly brushed, each metal-gray strand in its place. He waited patiently for a girl in a serape and blue jeans to get out of his way, then went back the aisle to the rear of the room, walking with dignity, not looking at anyone. Barry stared at the man's back. *If only. If only Dr. Thayer would take over.* But, staring, dazed, Barry realized sluggishly that it was the day of his first lecture, his first teaching attempt, *his* class-period, and that everyone was staring at him and no one else, at *him.* Though he dreaded moving, because of the possibility of being sick, he went to the door and closed it. It made a loud noise. Someone giggled and Barry realized, too late, that he had lost his chance to walk out: he had been right there, by the door, and had not run out. *Now he was trapped.* That was why someone giggled and why, before him in the lecture-hall, big hulking grinning boys were watching closely for him to faint. It was so strange, the silence in this room. Most of the time, even during Thayer's lectures, there was an undertone of whispering and mumbling.

Now they were all staring, as if waiting for a play to begin.

Barry went back to the podium, noticing how long it took him to get there. His legs were rather numb. He could feel himself walking across the room, and everyone watching, staring, and just as he passed some contraption—it was a gigantic television set perched atop a portable scaffolding, for use in other classes—he stumbled over a cord and noticed how they all drew in their breaths, sharply, waiting for him to fall. When he got to the podium he opened one of the books at random, then, his eyesight blotching a little, he took out the sheaf of notes he'd prepared and looked at them. He frowned at them, so that the students would think all was well. Actually, he could not see for half-seconds at a time . . . then, when he could make out a word, he did not understand what the word was. The room was quite silent now. At the very back, in the desk Barry usually sat in, Dr. Thayer was seated, his arms folded. He was so far away that Barry could not read his expression.

"Today— Today— Today—"

Barry paused and began again. His voice had been rather weak. He pitched it a little higher and said, "Today I am going to talk about, about, a hotly-contested problem of ownership, I mean authorship. . . . The subject for today is. . . ." He licked his lips and squinted at the first sentence of his notes. Something about Shakespeare's imagery . . . a controversial case made by one scholar about the iterative imagery in the late plays. . . . But Barry didn't know what this was: evidently this belonged at the back of his sheaf of notes? He took another page out of the pile and began reading the first paragraph, in a voice so shrill and yet so determined that a few students began to take notes, automatically. He was reading off something about the four main principles one must utilize in the difficult art of handwriting analysis. . . . He did all right until something happened: the door opened and a girl hurried in, late, and slammed the door behind her and then, gaping at him, exclaimed that she was in the wrong class—wasn't she?— then, hitting the side of her face in an exaggerated theatrical way, she said *"Oh you're the TA"* and everyone laughed. She made her way to a vacant seat somewhere in the middle of the room. Barry stared at her. Then he wasn't seeing her, or seeing anything at all. He just stood there, staring into space. After a while it got very quiet again. There was a nauseous cloud distributed equally in all the parts of his body, even in his mouth and eyes, and he did not dare move suddenly. Yet they were waiting for him to move! A boy's head swam somewhere in the far right corner of Barry's vision, a head confused with long tawny stringy hair and a pair of aviator sunglasses, one ear exposed to show a golden earring, then the head blurred away and another face, quite close to Barry, horribly close, in the very first row, moved into sharp focus: a tough-looking girl, or maybe it was a boy, who wore a university

126

sweatshirt and was staring at Barry quite contemptuously. *Well?*

"The problem . . . the general problem. . . . There is a problem. . . . It has been a hotly-contested problem," Barry mumbled, not knowing why someone laughed, out there in the blur; then he had the sudden thought that perhaps a great space of time had passed, and he craned his head around to look at the clock—and it was only six minutes after eleven. *Six minutes after eleven!* He would have guessed that it was nearly eleven-thirty. This so staggered him that he forgot even to complete his sentence, he couldn't exactly recall how the sentence had begun, anyway, and so he said, going on to the next part of his lecture, "If you have any questions about this you can see me after class," and then, faintly, feebly, something in the sound of his own voice encouraged him and he said, attempting a smile, "Well, if Shakespeare was alive it would matter, but he isn't, is he, most of them aren't . . . from that time . . . most of them are dead . . . and Sturgess . . . all six of them are dead. . . . The subject for today is tragedy. . . . The syllabus says *Hamlet.* . . . I, uh, I didn't get to read the play last night . . . I. . . . Uh, the real thing is," he said. He stared out at the faces. They were absolutely silent, waiting. The classroom had never been so silent before. ". . . I formed my own theory about Shakespeare and Sturgess," he said. At that moment, eerily, he seemed to have formed a theory. He went on, vaguely, ". . . that one of them was a pseudonym for the other . . . and then somebody came along and erased the word . . . the name . . . and then the other name . . . both of the names." He swallowed. He saw them glancing at one another, not in derision as usual but in alarm, then he could see nothing, no one, and had grabbed from somewhere a piece of chalk. This made him feel better at once. He said, "The subject for today is tragedy. The subject for today is *Hamlet. Hamlet,* tragedy, Hamlet, what was his problem, he was uh what age, uh, if the subject is tragedy—" And here he got an idea: he wrote the word *tragedy* on the board. Some of the students automatically wrote it down in their notebooks. This encouraged him, so he smiled and said, with a sudden peculiar stab of excitement, "Shakespeare is dead but we're alive, he wouldn't mind, why should he

127

mind?—*drive your cart over the bones of the dead!*—he didn't say that—or did he?—who said that?—someone else said *Let the dead bury the dead!*—what was Hamlet's problem?—how the hell did he end up dead, I mean why was it so crazy back there, he was our age and, uh, wasn't he?—and what was so tragic about him or it or what was the thing they were trying to get through to?— Was it anything you could avoid? I mean, what was the tragedy of it?—what is tragedy?—*what is tragedy?*"

He turned back to them, the chalk in his hand, and from somewhere blurrily, cloudily, a memory of a professor he'd had years ago rose in him: a man sitting on the edge of a table, his foot dangling, smoking a cigarette and asking them questions, and Barry heard himself asking a question in that professor's voice, even raising his forehead as that professor had raised his. *"What the hell is tragedy about?"* The boy with the earring put his hand up and said, excitedly, that *he* thought it was about a bunch of people in some kingdom where the king ran everything and the main thing he could make out, he said, now stammering, the main thing was— was—that they all ended up dead. A few students laughed at this. No one had ever spoken up in the class before, because Dr. Thayer did not allow student commentary, and Barry stared smiling at the boy with the earring and thinking *Well Christ, he's worse off than I am,* and he made a joke and said yes, well right, well fine, but why did they end up dead?—a girl raised her hand hesitantly but lowered it again and Barry heard himself saying that it didn't matter if Shakespeare was dead, did it, because things were still pretty tragic, weren't they, and did any of them know what it was like to be Hamlet, had any of them gone through that kind of a mess?— and some of the students nodded so vehemently that Barry didn't dare call on them, for fear of losing the class's attention, because he knew now what he wanted to say: he wanted to give them his theory of tragedy.

So he wrote on the blackboard the word *freedom,* beside the other word.

And he went on to talk to them, excitedly, brokenly, that it was all about wanting to be free, that that was the hell of it, that in the past all those people, those suffering people like Hamlet and the others, they had wanted to be *free* . . . but everybody held them down, a lot of old dead dying bastards held them down . . . and it was still going on, but now people knew better, because they could read *Hamlet* and, and get what out of it?—what wisdom out of it? Not that you wind up dead, Barry went on, jabbing at the blackboard with his piece of chalk, not every goddam time you don't, but sometimes you did, and that was what tragedy was and that was why they read it and Hamlet's problem in his opinion was that he didn't run like hell to some other country when the ghost showed up. . . . Let the dead bury the dead! Let the old man tunnel around like a mole! It was really awful, it was hell, in fact the old king said he was in purgatory and suffering there, okay, that was probably something very bad psychologically for him, but Hamlet had his own life ahead of him . . . but . . . but how could he get to be free, how could he break out of the tragedy closing in on him?

"How can we all break out of it?" Barry asked passionately.

They argued about this and Barry got so excited he leafed through the big Shakespeare anthology to find the play, why the hell hadn't he marked the play, but he found it and skimmed along till he came to a passage he somehow remembered—magically, incredibly—he had not read this play since his sophomore year at U-M but he remembered exactly the speech he needed— Hamlet's last words, which he read to the class, forcing his voice to calm down, to resist exaggeration: *You that look pale and tremble at this chance, that are but mutes or audience to this act, had I but time— oh I could tell you—but let it be—I am dead, thou livest.*

That was the secret meaning of that play, and of all tragedy— *I am dead, thou livest.* He told them it was the most important thing they would learn in this course or in their entire lives and that they *must* learn it, or they would be in a tragedy too. And Barry heard his voice as if from a distance, now calmed down, not crazily excited . . . he had slid into a moment of great emotion and great beauty, not knowing until the very instant of his entering it of what power it had, a power almost outside him, not to be resisted.

*   *   *   *

At the end of the class he gathered his books and notes together —what was all this?—all this?—aware of Dr. Thayer approaching the front of the room, slowly, very slowly. The last of the students had trooped out. And there Dr. Thayer stood, near the door, looking toward Barry. He held the tape-recorder in his arms, tightly, and stood as if prepared to defend himself: how slyly and maliciously he smiled at Barry! Barry stuffed everything into his bookbag and walked out. He passed near Thayer, walking out, not even bothering to look at him. The hell with Thayer, the hell with all of them. Something was dead but something else was living. . . . So, he would be dropped from the Hilberry program? Very well, then, he would be dropped. And return to the States and apply for welfare? Maybe. He did not care. Dropped from the graduate program or not dropped, Barry with an advanced degree or without an advanced degree, what did it matter?

Life was drama, not to be resisted. What had it to do with these problems, these books and notes and slips of green paper? What had any of this to do with him? Thayer had flashed Barry a cold, furious, level, insane look—he was insane, yes—yet somehow sane, in control. It was that small kernel of sanity that was so terrifying.

REWARDS OF FAME

The airliner did not crash, as he had somehow expected. Incredibly, it got to its meager, forgettable destination—Kitimit, Iowa—ten minutes ahead of schedule.

Murray Licht was the first off, elbowing his way along, muttering apologies, excuses, clearing a pathway with his fake-alligator skin briefcase; he felt muscles reviving in him that he had imagined were atrophied, after the nine—was it only nine?—days of this trip. There were friendly, expectant Midwestern faces waiting for passengers to get off the plane, and Murray was shrewd enough to hurry past them without exactly looking at them. Maybe he was recognized; maybe not. But in a dizzyingly-brief span of time, mere seconds, he was safe inside the terminal, safe inside a telephone booth, and reaching in his pocket for some change—what, was it mostly pennies?—somehow when he travelled he became weighted down, rattling with small change—and sighing with relief, able to dial her number, direct, before anyone hurried up to him and said, *Aren't you Murray Licht . . . ?*

Far away, back across the continent, in New York: her telephone rang, was ringing, ringing firmly and hopefully. . . . He listened to it eagerly, expecting each ring to be the last; then he'd hear her voice and all would be well. Four, five, six heroic rings. . . . Now he noticed them searching for him. Yes, there they were, his welcoming committee, evidently; they were actually scouting for him, grim-faced, frowning, even a little frightened. He had walked right past them without hesitating, and they hadn't dared to say hello, or maybe they'd been confused by the determined way he had rushed by. Or maybe he no longer resembled his publicity photographs.

His hand cupped over the receiver, he turned slightly aside, so that if they happened to discover him it would seem quite natural —Murray Licht was making an important call back home, checking with someone, perhaps letting an interested party know that he had landed safely in Kitimit, Iowa. Yes, that would seem natural to them. The three men looked like ordinary decent youngish middle-aged men, associate professors, probably; they could see the point of telephone calls back home.

. . . eleven, twelve rings. . . .

He hung up in despair. No use, she must be out for the day, already . . . or perhaps she was staying away from the apartment for some reason. It had grown to have "morbid associations," she said, without explaining what she meant. Coins rattled in the telephone, then sank. Murray forced a laugh, a practice laugh at his own distress. *Fifty-year-old fiancé of beautiful young heiress laughs at own distress. . . .*

He left the telephone booth and they saw him. Now. Now they closed in upon him, eyebrows raised, their smiles boyish and hopeful—*Aren't you Murray Licht?*

"Hello, hello," he said, with a big smile.

Handshakes. Introductions. One of them would say, predictably: "Mr. Licht, I'm Brian Fuller, who's been corresponding with you— how do you do?—we hope you had a smooth trip from St. Louis— wasn't it St. Louis?—now, uh, everything is arranged at the Inn and we'll take you there right away—everything should be set— Excitement on campus has grown almost to a fever pitch—there's real enthusiasm among the students and, and the faculty both— Should we—? My car is outside, we'd better leave—it's eleven-twenty, now, exactly—and we don't have too much time—the luncheon is at 1:00— We hope you had a smooth pleasant flight, Mr. Licht—"

The inevitable station wagon: its back part cluttered with children's toys and overshoes and miscellaneous domestic items. Somehow, Murray had the distinct feeling of having ridden in this station wagon before.

But he knew he had not been to Lapointe College before. He was positive of that. Lapointe was his fourth stop in the past nine days, and it was new to him, it had to be new to him; these pleasant, slightly edgy men were strangers; it was only an eerie coincidence that they happened to be chattering about the same things, asking him the same questions, he'd heard at his most recent stop, in Missouri. The advantage of the situation was that he could reply without thinking, so that he was free to concentrate on the cause of his misery this morning. Yes. *Yes.* He and Rosalind were going to be married on the Saturday following the completion of his spring poetry-reading tour. They had discussed the basic outline of their future together, solemnly, repeatedly, and the date of the wedding was an irrevocable one: June 2. However, since the day before yesterday he had been unable to make contact with her. A terrible rainstorm had been following him around the Midwest—a part of the United States he disliked and feared and, for some reason, felt he could not understand—and it seemed to him, superstitiously, that this had something to do with his failure to reach her.

She was living quietly and secretly in a small apartment a few miles from Vassar, where her ex-husband taught psychology; he didn't know she had moved back. He was her second husband: the first had been an older man, exactly how old Murray had never wanted to know, who had died of a coronary attack after only eight months of marriage. Rosalind, a young widow, had unwisely—as she analyzed it—married again, almost at once, this time a quite young man who was brilliant, yes, but far too immature, really "undeveloped." That marriage had deteriorated quickly. So Rosalind—a tall, sharp-faced, beautiful young woman of 27—arranged for a divorce, aided by her father, under newer and far more liberal divorce laws than her father had enjoyed for *his,* a decade earlier. Rosalind's father was one of Rockefeller's aides and spent most of his time at the state capitol; meetings set up between him and Murray always seemed to fall through, though he had evidently read some of Murray's poetry and "gave his approval" of the marriage.

After the divorce Rosalind had shipped all her furniture and belongings to a farmhouse outside Norfolk, Virginia, having rented it sight unseen through an advertisement in the *New York Times*; she had wanted—as she explained to Murray the first evening of their acquaintance, in her tearful, self-accusatory voice—to "purify her mind of the vicious past." But the Norfolk farmhouse had not worked out: too isolated, oppressive. She had had nothing to do there but think about the past. And so she'd moved everything back to New York City, to a ground floor apartment in the Village, a brownstone owned by a supposed friend of hers and her ex-husband's; but the friend had become a tenant-exploiting landlord, he'd given up all pretensions of being a composer, and again, once again, poor lovely jittery Rosalind had had to move: to a women's hotel in Manhattan, and finally back out to Poughkeepsie, where she felt safe. Murray had met her just as she was moving out of the brownstone. He himself lived in Manhattan, but because of difficulties with his wife he sometimes lived on Long Island—it was a complicated set of relationships and he frequently forgot its details —and, though he had pressed Rosalind to move in with him, in Westbury, she had insisted upon remaining independent until the wedding. There was a massive weedy garden out back of her apartment building and she liked to work in it, hour after hour. So: maybe that's where she was, in her yellow linen slacks that fanned at the ankles, weeding, endlessly weeding, beads of perspiration on her forehead as the telephone rang and rang and she seemed never to hear it. . . .

"Mr. Licht—?"

"Yes, yes?"

"—quite a hectic day ahead of all of us!—hope you don't mind that we've added a little extra session, just an informal meeting with some very interested *very* well-read and sharp students—"

"Call me Murray, please," he said, as they herded him along a plastic-canopied walk and into the lobby of a motel—the Lapointe Motor Inn—which was so new that construction hadn't yet been completed, on one of the side wings. Murray wanted only to escape from them; he *must* get to a telephone before this long day of scheduled luncheons and readings and conversations seriously began. The brusque big-jawed farm-boyish Bobbie Sutter—evidently Lapointe's poet-in-residence—asked the desk clerk for "the Licht room," and Murray found himself playing the role of Murray Licht, *the* clever sardonic warm-at-heart bearish-elegant Licht, whose poetry had been called both urbane and tragic, in the tradition of Rilke—joking with the clerk (who muttered something about the maid almost being finished with that floor, he'd check to make sure) and Brian Fuller and the other man, whose name he'd already forgotten—Hardy, was it?—or had Hardy been one of the professors at an earlier stop, in Indiana?—Murray in absolute control of his own trembling hands and rather flattered at the way these two men studied him, absurdly reverential, as if they were trying to memorize his words or were trying, at this very moment, to reconstruct them into an anecdote of some kind. *Murray Licht isn't at all what you think. . . .* Or maybe: *Murray Licht is exactly what you think!*

The "Licht room" was not yet ready, but another room would do as well, Murray insisted, so they herded him along a mile and a half of newly-carpeted corridors that smelled of concrete-dust. They even came into the room with him, checking it to make sure it was good enough—"We've been a little disappointed with the Inn in the past," they said—and it was five minutes to twelve before Murray was alone. He could have wept, he was so frustrated.

They were coming to get him, they said, at twelve-thirty sharp.

Murray picked up the telephone receiver at once, but hesitated, and dialed Room Service. He asked for a martini, but the woman said words that seemed to add up to "no," so he asked for a bottle of beer, and then, after a few complicated moments of dialogue it developed that the Room Service girl was explaining the county laws about alcoholic beverages: something about times of day, days of the week. "Thank you, thank you," he said, and hung up.

He poured himself a drink—he had a bottle in his suitcase—and returned to the telephone with renewed enthusiasm. But he was so rigorously introspective, so relentlessly self-conscious ("a poetic imagination that rarely settles for seductive but simple-minded optimism") that he distrusted his own enthusiasm. The situation was this: at the Holiday Inn near the airport, last night in St. Louis, he had drunk so much, alone, that he'd collapsed fully-clothed, with his shoes on, not even on the king-sized lonely bed but on the carpet, overcome with the terror (it was almost an intellectual, logical terror) that if Rosalind continued not to answer the telephone. . . . he would be unable to continue this poetry-reading tour. He would break down, he'd have to cancel his appearances. It had happened once before—in 1964—in the midst of the transitional period between Helga (his second wife) and the still-married, undecided Marilyn (who was to become his third wife, eventually). He had made enemies on that trip who still hated him, and who were perhaps lying in wait for him. . . . But it was best not to think of that.

So, instead of risking the humiliation of another unanswered call, he decided to look through the mimeographed announcements and schedules Brian Fuller had given him. Evidently it was "Iowa Poetry Week." He skimmed most of it and located "Murray Licht," reading from his poetry at 4 P.M. in the Ogg Memorial Center. Yes, he knew he was scheduled to give a reading at 4. But other items in the program were new to him. He hadn't bothered to read Fuller's letters all the way through, or maybe he had confused Lapointe with Loudin, a small college in Philadelphia, his first stop on the tour; he did not seem to remember that the Lapointe stop-over was part of a symposium. It looked as if an old friend-enemy, Harmon Orbach, had given a reading the day before, in the Ogg Memorial Center, at 4 P.M. Orbach! He hadn't seen him since a disastrous poetry panel at Michigan a few years ago. Murray had done well as usual (he was quite professional when in good health) but Orbach had antagonized an alliance of black students and Gay Liberation people, because of one of his poems, or a single line in one of his poems. Orbach was about 46 now; he had the reputation of being weak, mild-mannered, "mystical," having spent some time in Ceylon and India, and he did appear almost saintly in his rough-textured robes and sandals. When he removed his glasses, on stage, his eyes were enlarged and vulnerable. Because he loved everyone he could not reason how certain people disliked him: this made him furious. It was Murray's private theory that Orbach was actually insane. . . . He dreaded meeting him again.

But worse than that, Lapointe's "special poet-in-residence" this week was a woman poet, Hannah Dominic—whom Murray had met only a few times, and really detested. Orbach was at least a poet, but Hannah Dominic was not. She was not a poet, she was a shouter, a journalist-in-verse, and remarkably young when you considered her reputation: not yet thirty. Murray poured a little more Scotch into the glass, uneasily. He was not afraid of the Dominic woman, but he did hope she hadn't read the review he had written of one of her books. . . how could she have missed it, though, since it had been in the *New York Times?*. . . . he couldn't remember it clearly himself, not even the exact title of the book . . . it had been an omnibus review and he hadn't had time to finish reading all the books under review. . . . *Shrieks? Whispers?* A typically strident, hysterical title like that. . . . But worse than this, at 8 that evening something called the William Randolph Hearst Memorial Lecture would be given, in the Science Auditorium, by Joachim Myer— "the internationally-prominent critic and man of letters"—and here Murray began to feel real horror, for Joachim had not only lost, temporarily, a girl Rhodes Scholar to Murray, many years ago, but the two of them had been co-editors of a literary magazine at Columbia, as undergraduates. They had feared and avoided each other for years, and the title of Myer's talk was *What Was Poetry?*

Though he had only a few minutes remaining, Murray went to take a quick, cold shower. It was a ritual Rosalind had taught him, a way of inducing calm through shock, the total obliteration of the ego.

He was picked up at twelve-thirty sharp, not by Fuller this time but by a young woman and another man, both "involved in the creative writing program," as they explained, assistant professors in the department. The woman drove, chattering excitedly. She

139

handled the stick-shift of the Volkswagen with a dexterity that made Murray—who didn't drive at all—very nervous. He clutched his briefcase, required out of politeness to keep meeting the woman's friendly glance and to nod, grateful that he could not manage to get a word in, with all that chatter, but worried about whether she, like so many other bright hectic young women of her type, scattered throughout the academic world, would expect some bizarre offer from him. He had to be cautious. He hadn't the aplomb of Richie James, the freewheeling Florida poet who didn't mind how he was discussed and judged and maybe laughed over, even alluded to in classrooms by women who had befriended him on his poetry-reading tours; nor had he the reputation of icy chastity contrived by S. W. Martin, who was so cerebral, so handsomely and priggishly aloof, that nothing more was expected of him than that he tolerate academicians' flattery and autograph a few books. *He* was *Murray Licht. . . .*

But he didn't always know what that meant. What did it mean? Friends told him that his behavior confused women, because he gave the impression of being robustly flirtatious, and when he had had a few drinks he was quite charming, they said; but in fact Murray had been attracted to no more than half a dozen women in his adult life, and these he had pursued, truly pursued, in an obsessive, heroic way. The women, including Rosalind, had all been elusive, indifferent at first, even a little hostile toward him . . . they came to love him eventually but as a kind of surrender, a giving up of defenses. He was unable to take seriously any woman who seemed interested in him, and certainly he could not stand any woman who claimed to admire his poetry. Still, there were stray uncontrollable rumors about him . . . really inaccurate, misleading, but he had no way of correcting them. He had lost any helpful awareness, years ago, of who or what "Licht" was reputed to be, other than, of course, a vague disappointment to the critics who had —God, how many decades ago!—claimed him as a genius, in the tradition of Rilke; these were the really important, intelligent critics, whose judgment Murray knew to be correct. Yes, he realized he was a shambling entertaining failure by now, he knew from the inside that something had gone wrong with his poetry—with him—but he didn't know, had never known, to what extent this assessment was shared by the rest of the country. In spite of his big-chested big-voiced manner Murray had an intellectual integrity about himself: he was not hypocritical, was not a fraud. Yet he worried that it might seem impolite to interrupt huge lava-like streams of praise—the young woman beside him was still talking—or to cry *Shut up! Leave me alone! Stop that mockery!*

At the doorway to the special banquet room of the Ogg Center was a sign: *English Dept. Luncheon 1 p.m.—2 p.m.* Murray was herded in by Sandy Michaels (that was the young woman's name) and the other assistant professor, a bearded young man who looked no more than nineteen, named Smitty or Scottie, and introduced to a group of people who shook his hand energetically and claimed to be *very* honored. . . . An older man who called himself Professor Stone apologized for the fact that someone wasn't there . . . a string of names that meant nothing to Murray . . . and it was a pity, the departmental chairman was off somewhere on a fund-raising campaign with the vice-chancellor . . . but he was interrupted by Bobbie Sutter who said that there was a fever-pitch of excitement among the students, building up all semester, but how frustrating it was, three brilliant poets crammed into four days!. . . .

"That Dominic woman is *really* something," Fuller marvelled.

Murray felt a little panicked. But, as always at such times, he was carried along by the external harmless frenzy of his hosts, the fuss over seating arrangements, missing napkins, people rushing in two minutes late and apologizing profusely, as if their absences had been a matter of alarmed conversation. . . . Only after they were all seated and things calmed down a little, might he begin to feel uneasy.

Then a lovely young woman entered the room—remarkably like Rosalind, quite tall, with high cheekbones, her dark hair feathery and gleaming—but, thank God, she was only a student waitress; he wouldn't have to stare moronically at her for very long. . . . He found himself seated between Fuller and Bobbie Sutter, and gathered from the course of the conversation, from embarrassed halts and ellipses, that something had gone wrong. Of course: neither Harmon Orbach nor Hannah Dominic was here, at the luncheon. Murray felt absurdly hurt. There were more than two places vacant, however . . . Murray counted at least eight at the table.

"Scottie tried to contact Orbach out at the Inn, but evidently . . . somehow. . . . Last night, at Dr. Preston's house . . . a dinner party . . . some disagreement between Miss Dominic and Orbach . . . arguing over a young woman poet . . . the name wasn't familiar to the rest of us. . . . If they don't come to the luncheon in your honor, Mr. Licht, it isn't anything personal, we are all sure, we *know*, they both want very much to meet you. . . ." Fuller said, but his painful remarks were interrupted by Bobbie's energetic voice: "That's what's wonderful about poetry in America!—so many divergent currents, democratic voices!—a cross-current of dia-logues!" but it was Professor Stone, white-haired, creased, with an uninsistent unemphatic monotone of a voice, who broke through everyone else: "This is *Poetry Week* in Iowa! And the student paper and the *Kitimit Herald* are both doing extensive features— we've triumphed over a great deal of controversy between those of us who believe—nay, who have dedicated our lives to the principle —that art is much more than regional, that it *must* be more than regional!—between us and those who claim that Iowa Poetry Week should be for Iowa poets alone! And you and Mr. Orbach and Miss Dominic and, of course, Joachim Myer, are our living proof— our proof of—of—" Here he broke off, his eyes watering.

Evidently there were no drinks at the luncheon. So it moved along rather swiftly, and Murray decided against asking these people—attracting the attention of all 15 of them—why in God's name they had invited that showman-maniac Joachim Myer?—to give a talk called *What Was Poetry?*—but the question might only have stymied them ("But isn't Joachim Myer a prominent man of letters . . . ?") and caused confusion. Also, he didn't really want to know. He could overhear Miss Michaels' loud voice somewhere to the left of him, *As we drove over here we were saying . . . Mr. Licht said . . . I asked him, and . . . I told him about our. . . .* but his attention was drawn to the girl waitress again, who brought him

142

his club sandwich plate (both Fuller and Sutter had recommended it, since it came with a large side-dish of French fries). She set it before him, she said nothing, did not seem to hear his grateful *Thank you!* and set identical plates before Fuller and Sutter, as if they were all alike, perhaps she was not an English major and had never heard of Murray Licht . . . ? He watched her walk away, his eyes filling with moisture, like Professor Stone's, as he thought again of Rosalind and how she might elude him, after all their vows and plans and the lease they had actually signed, co-signed, on a wonderful weatherbeaten Cape Cod home out on Long Island. Since his twenties he had pursued these beautiful women, had pushed himself beyond the usual physical limitations of his type (large-boned but unmuscular, with curiously thin legs), like a hiker taking on unmapped territory, he had failed to develop his poetry, had failed utterly to become the Murray Licht he felt he was destined to be . . . and now, at an age he could not quite believe in . . . he might no longer have the endurance, the psychological recklessness needed to match his imagination. . . . But such thoughts depressed him, they were dangerous; so he was grateful when the girl disappeared and he could concentrate on the fragmented conversation at his end of the table, remarks and queries about a rumored scandal involving the National Book Awards this year . . . was it true? . . . Murray, who knew that most scandals, rumored or unrumored, were true, shook his head gravely and said he didn't think so, no, the people who handled such things were always above suspicion. That tamed them. They switched, contritely, to their own students and to the pitch of excitement that had been building since January—"No, since last fall!" someone corrected—and though Murray didn't care to hear about Hannah Dominic's "very successful" reading and her "wonderful popularity" with the undergraduate girls, he had to seem intigued: he couldn't tell these good people that Hannah Dominic wasn't a poet, that her "poems" were just trashy prose invectives against the male sex, and her temporary popularity was itself an aberration. . . .

The eight vacant places at the luncheon table never filled up; in fact, an older woman professor at the other end of the table left early, without saying any special goodbye to Murray. He felt hurt. And he couldn't help noticing that, with the exception of Professor Stone, the older members of the department were talking among themselves and, if they bothered to look at Murray, they didn't seem to show that alert curious respect the younger staff showed. Fuller, Sutter, Sandy Michaels, and "Scottie" were conferring about whether they should tell Murray about someone named Dr. Lyndon, and Sutter finally said: "Something unusual happened at Harmon Orbach's reading yesterday . . . and there isn't the slightest chance of its being repeated at yours . . . but. . . . One of our department members, Dr. Lyndon, our Swift scholar . . . you've probably heard of him . . . no? . . . well, he's quite conservative and outspoken and . . . and rather critical. . . . He's a fine scholar, a very valuable man, but rather critical. . . . In fact, he was even critical of the last poet we had here for a reading, how long ago was that, Brian? . . . gee, it must have been three-four years already! . . . it was Stephen Spender. Well, Dr. Lyndon didn't approve of him either, but he was fairly polite, nothing like the way he was with poor Mr. Orbach yesterday. . . ."

"Tim Lyndon doesn't mean half of what he says!" Professor Stone laughed. "Not the destructive part, anyway! I've known him for forty years!"

". . . yes, that's true. . . . He did embarrass your friend Mr. Orbach a little, yesterday, in fact he sat in the very front row with a boy who is doing a thesis with him, an M.A. thesis on Swift's high standards of morality . . . and the two of them interrupted Orbach's very first poem, a sutra, I believe he called it, and asked him some complicated question about metrics. When Mr. Orbach didn't know the answer, in terms of his own poetry, the reading became very confused . . . and it was unfortunate . . . unfortunate that. . . ."

"Did you know that Harmon Orbach has a stammer?" Sandy asked Murray. "He has a stammer."

"I didn't know Harmon had a stammer, no, not necessarily," Murray said. He felt as if he were sailing off into a dream. Professor Stone leaned over to tap his arm and to assure him that Tim

144

Lyndon didn't mean half of what he said—in fact, sometimes he didn't mean anything of what he said—he was near retirement age, that was it. "Maybe he won't bother with my reading," Murray said shakily.

"Oh I don't think he will!" someone said. "He wouldn't dare, not after yesterday—"

"Oh yes, the Dean is furious. The incident got into the *Herald*—"

Brian Fuller, sucking at a pipe, interrupted them in order to make a small speech he might have been composing all this time. "What we want you to realize, to know, Mr. Licht, is that those of us who planned this symposium—since last July, in fact—those of us in the creative writing program, and many, *many* students, are all solidly behind you. And the other poets. And if a few older members of our department seem a little cool and, you know, unfriendly, it isn't anything personal."

"Some of them hate the creative writing program," Bobbie Sutter said, his voice not so boyish as usual. In fact he sounded vicious. "The old bastard Lyndon hates us all and wants to destroy us . . . when the Senate voted to put everyone on one-year renewable contracts . . . because of our enrollment drop . . . the old bastard ran up the aisle and started shouting about tenure, and how younger staff members should be fired right away. . . ."

"Why Bobbie," Brian Fuller said, alarmed. "Mr. Licht doesn't want to hear about something that happened 'way last September!"

Though Murray and a few of the others were not quite finished with their jello desserts, the luncheon ended abruptly: the Ogg Center staff quit work at two and the table had to be cleared at once.

*   *   *   *

Murray hoped for a few stolen minutes to himself, even in a lavatory somewhere. But no: next on the agenda was a brief guided tour of the college. He was ushered out of the Ogg Center, this time wedged between Professor Stone and Miss Michaels, who each seemed to want to point out important sights to him. The other professors had dwindled to three, then to two: then only Professor

Stone and Miss Michaels and Murray remained. "That facade is an exact reproduction of the original facade of Fort Kitimit, destroyed in 1883, an Indian uprising that killed hundreds of men," Professor Stone was saying, as they passed the Administration Building—Murray knew nothing about architecture except to know when a building looked old, or "colonial," and this did—though it was handsome enough, ivy-covered like all the rest—and Miss Michaels kept tugging at his sleeve and making wry witticisms he didn't quite catch—God, was he going deaf?—though he had the idea she was making fun of Professor Stone. He liked Professor Stone.

They spent some time by the statue of General Lapointe, which Professor Stone explained was the "finest example of the sculptor Hendricks' work"; Hendricks was Iowa's outstanding sculptor. Murray said it was "handsome and solid"—causing Miss Michaels to giggle appreciatively, as though he had said something obscene, while in fact he had been speaking more or less sincerely, as he usually did. He was becoming irritated with the woman and wanted only to escape . . . though next on the agenda was the meeting with creative writing students in a place called Cameron Hall. They led him there, across the college's quadrangle, which was called a "green," and Murray saw that the college was charming, yes, pastoral and peaceful and lovely. . . . If only . . . ! If only his life had turned out differently . . . ! Perhaps *this* was the world he should have tried for. Here, somewhere in the Midwest, so far from New York City that one could forget it permanently, he and Tanya, his first wife, could have bought a house . . . he'd be a full professor by now, respected by everyone . . . perhaps he would share an office with Professor Stone, or Tim Lyndon . . . all old friends, old colleagues. . . .

Why hadn't that happened?

They got him to Cameron Hall a few minutes early. Bobbie Sutter was chatting with students in a big lecture hall, boys and girls who looked very young. Murray saw only one long-haired glittery-eyed boy, who reminded him horribly of his eldest son, now in his late twenties, whom he hadn't seen for several years . . . that boy

146

looked intelligent, at least; maybe he would ask provocative questions. The others seemed very shy. Finally, Bobbie said that it looked as if no one else was coming, he might as well introduce Mr. Licht—"who needs no introduction!"—though Sandy Michaels interrupted to ask in a whisper whether they shouldn't move to a smaller room?—because of the funny acoustics in here?—but Murray said he didn't mind, this was fine with him, it was great, great. There were about 20 students in the room, but for some reason they were scattered out among 100 or 150 seats, which rose in tiers. . . . To play down his own nervousness, Murray joked and said something about poetry in a post-literate age, how many in the room hoped to be poets? . . . so many! . . . well yes . . . good . . . he joked a little more, aimlessly, relying upon his own voice to fill up the stark silence of the lecture hall, waiting for the first question. Most of the students looked baffled and shy; a boy with a crewcut, sitting near the door, got up and slipped out. He was followed by another boy, whose shoes squeaked. But finally the long-haired boy lifted his hand. He asked an extremely complicated question—almost a speech—and Murray was grateful simply for its length. It involved Licht's conception of himself as a "literary force" in "opposition" to the current "mainstream" represented by Hannah Dominic: would he comment?

"Gladly," Murray said. He had no idea what the question meant; but he could answer anything, he was perfectly at home dealing with abstractions, with words; in fact he felt, here in Cameron Hall, really good for the first time that day. He wouldn't have to think about the French fries he had eaten, so unwisely, or about lovely weeping Rosalind, or about the mysterious failure of Licht as he was known back home—he wouldn't have to think about anything, in fact. He could answer students' questions.

*   *   *   *

The session went surprisingly well.

Murray wished he could remember what he said at such times, since people often complimented him on being so articulate, so "good at fielding questions"; but he always forgot. Bobbie Sutter came forward to shake his hand, thanking him for all the help he'd given these students, how wonderful it was for them to come into contact with a real poet—and here were the ten final contestants' poems, in a manila envelope—"of course we've asked them to use pseudonyms," Bobbie explained. Murray, perspiring, feeling a little drained after the hour-and-a-half session, didn't let on that he had no idea what these poems were . . . though he gathered, from Bobbie's conversation as they walked across the quad to the bookstore (next on the agenda was a supervised visit to the bookstore and "Mr. Casey," the manager, a wonderful fellow) that Lapointe was sponsoring a poetry contest for undergraduates. The results were to be announced at the banquet that evening. "So as soon as you get a free hour or so, you could maybe arrange them in order of excellence," Bobbie said.

Mr. Casey was a bald, wizened, lively man of an indeterminate age, who pumped Murray's hand and seemed delighted to meet him "at last." He took him on a lengthy, narrated tour of the bookstore ("For fifteen years we had to operate out of the basement of Prentiss, and now look!—so much space!"), ending with the display of the Visiting Poets' Books. Murray was touched, the display was so large and well-intentioned, decorated with glossy photographs of himself and Orbach (as he looked twenty years ago) and Hannah Dominic (who looked young and ghastly—sickly, ascetic, with a thin-lipped evil smile that went through Murray like a razor), and stacks of their books. Mr. Casey was happy to report that Murray was "holding his own," though of course that Hannah Dominic was so popular!—and she'd been here since Tuesday, which made a difference. Murray counted only his first four books —where was *Cadences*, his most recent book? Mr. Casey mumbled something about the publisher not responding to his book orders. All of Harmon Orbach's four volumes were there, in soft covers, but it didn't look as if many had been sold. What a surprise, though, to see the number of books the Dominic woman had published already!—six, no seven—seven books of poetry, and she wasn't even thirty!—the prolific bitch. Murray was grateful for Orbach, who had only the four books and hadn't published any-

148

thing in years. It was well known that Orbach was finished, which was some consolation.

Murray picked up *Shrieks*, which had Hannah's picture on the cover, a witchy profile; yes, this was the book he'd been assigned to review. The dust jacket listed extremely favorable praise-paragraphs . . . two of the comments attributed to critics Murray halfway respected. Was everyone mad? Like nearly all reviewers, Murray set out to reward friends and punish enemies, though of course this necessarily involved, often, the rewarding of friends of friends and the punishing of friends of enemies. Hannah Dominic had fallen into the latter category. A few of her poems had been published by an editor who had, inexplicably, sent back some of Murray's poems . . . so he had written a brilliantly vicious review of *Shrieks*, one of the sharpest things he had done in years. He received many compliments on it. Afterward, when he came upon mention of Hannah Dominic, or heard that someone had met her, he felt vague alarm and resentment—somehow he'd thought he had finished her for good, had killed her. . . . But no: there she was, with her seven thick volumes of "prose-poems," ugly and aggressive and popular. Murray opened *Shrieks* at random, to read:

> with my dimestore stainless stained jackknife I sliced
> him open   he cried oh! don't do to me what I do to you
> he cried oh! don't let the maggots spill out

It was bad—hideous! He knew it was bad! He *knew!*

"Oh that Hannah Dominic, she's really something!" Mr. Casey marvelled. "Came in here yesterday to give me hell—she's so sincere and outspoken, you must admit—unusual qualities in a woman."

"What was she angry about?" Murray asked.

"Sharing the same counter with you and Orbach." Mr. Casey looked around for Bobbie Sutter, but Bobbie was browsing through magazines at the magazine rack, looking through *Playboy*. "It's nothing personal, Mr. Licht," Mr. Casey said, awkwardly, "at least I'm sure she likes you as a person . . . and I'm sure she admires your work, as everyone does. It's just that she's so hard to please. . . . Did they tell you she's been arousing the students against you? . . . to boycott your class session and reading? But I don't believe that our really serious students here at Lapointe, I mean the stable and sincere ones, you know, go along with that sort of thing. Just the neurotic ones. But you should know that Miss Dominic's attitude is not caused by anything personal against you."

"Not anything personal," Murray repeated.

"That's right," Mr. Casey said. "Nothing personal."

After the visit to the bookstore, Bobbie Sutter announced that Murray could rest now if he cared to. "In the privacy of my office," Bobbie said. Murray thanked him, weak with gratitude, and, left alone in Bobbie's office, felt for an instant that he would weep. He was so puzzled, so exhausted! . . . and there was a telephone, so he must call her . . . he must call her . . . though a failure to talk to her might destroy him, another failure, no, it was a risk he couldn't take . . . no, yes. . . . Yes. When he dialed "9," however, an operator informed him that all the outside lines were temporarily in use.

Relieved, he sat in a swivel chair, closed his eyes . . . then he leaned forward, thinking he would nap on Sutter's desk . . . but it was hard to find a comfortable position. The desk was a big aluminum desk and for some reason it seemed to be vibrating; at least, Murray could hear vibrations coming up through it. *Nothing personal, nothing personal . . .* he seemed to hear these words in the vibrations. A sharp pain reappeared in his right shoulder. *Christ,* Murray thought, *why am I here? . . . where am I? . . .* A few weeks ago Rosalind had taught him some hatha yoga positions (she took a course in yoga in Poughkeepsie, which was one of the reasons she wanted to live there) and in doing a difficult position called "the plow," which involved standing on his shoulders, so to speak, and lowering his legs slowly back over his face, he had somehow fallen sideways and the pain in his shoulder had been so awful, they'd both thought he might have dislocated it, at first. The throbbing had gradually faded but now it reappeared.

He didn't have time to nap, anyway. It was already twenty to four. He took advantage of the time to leaf through the students' poems and rearrange them quickly, trying not to actually see them,

though he could not stop himself from seeing the name—the pseudonym—on the topmost poem ("Shake S. Peare"). He stuffed
them all back in Bobbie's manila envelope and left it on his desk.
. . . Restless, he went to the window to look out. Sutter's office was
on the second floor of Cameron Hall, with a view of the green. It
was really an exceptionally charming campus. . . . And, except for
the cloudy, dangerous sky, the scene before him was striking:
flowering trees of some kind, pink and white and magenta (fruit
trees? lilacs? tulips?—he knew almost nothing about such things),
students strolling casually around, vivid fresh-green grass, newly-
mowed, everything innocent and serene. And how indifferent to his
presence, his agitated nerve-worn intellect! A small group was
leaving the college chapel, most of them older people, not students . . . there was a tall woman in black, wearing a black scarf
or mantilla (was that the term?—Murray knew little about Chris-
tian customs, though his last two wives had been gentiles), and he
wished absurdly that he had a pair of binoculars. She was closely
attended by an older man, who might have been a minister. The
mysterious group headed up one of the flat brick paths and were
obscured by flower-laden boughs.

After this it was impossible to settle down in Sutter's swivel
chair, and the broken-backed easy chair in a corner was out of the
question. Trembling with excitement Murray dialed the "9" again
and got an outside line—what good luck!—and dialed Rosalind's
number without hesitation. He did all this as gracefully as someone
in a film; while the phone rang at the other end he experienced an
odd thought, he wanted to ask Rosalind how old her father was. He
was a widower who looked so sporty, so healthy, that he seemed not
much older than Murray himself; but probably this was not the
case. The old man had a brown belt in karate and, though he was
a millionaire (most of the investments in Trans-World Steel) he
had always worked hard.

Where the hell was she? . . . the ringing went on and on, a con-
tinuation of the morning's relentless monotonous sound.

Twelve minutes to four! Those awful, smiling, good-hearted
people would come for him soon! . . . He would begin the reading

151

with a few love poems, written in honor of Rosalind; not his best poems, he knew, but he was fiercely proud of them, and had been infuriated when an old friend, an editor, had returned them with the comment that they weren't up to the high standards he had set himself "in the days of Helga." (Helga was his second wife.) But he intended to read them just the same. He had parted from Rosalind so long ago, it seemed . . . so long ago, though hardly more than a week . . . that already the circumstances of their farewell were blending into those of their initial meeting eight months before. So many of their evenings together were on neutral territory, as they called it: at a friend's Manhattan apartment, where a party had been held for a visiting English journalist whose editor was also the editor of one of Rosalind's closest friends, at the apartments and country houses and beach houses of Murray's friends, or the friends of his friends, who told him tales about his present wife's denunciation of him and his "heiress" fiancée. Sometimes they had met at the hotel-apartment building in Westbury, where Murray had been living for a few months, mainly because it was mid-way between his Manhattan brownstone (he wanted to visit his 13-year-old son, who had been expelled from two private schools this year and who couldn't get admitted to another) and the university he taught at, a new, high-rise school farther out on Long Island. As "poet-in-residence" he had only a one-year non-renewable contract but his teaching load was fairly light and the department chairman never seemed to mind, or to notice, when he went on reading tours. . . .

The telephone rang in Rosalind's neat, pretty, fully-carpeted apartment in Poughkeepsie. He wanted to scream at her. Was she cringing in the bathroom, afraid to answer the phone . . . ? Once, drunk, she had confessed to him that she had deliberately set out to attract her husband's brother, a nice boy her own age, had even "been affectionate" with him, whatever that meant, but then, afterward, forever afterward, never spoke to him or alluded to him. When she somehow sensed that he was telephoning her she hid in the bathroom, cringing, overcome with shame and guilt. *It's me, Murray, it isn't him!* he wanted to shout at her.

152

But of course he would forgive her. He had forgiven her many times already, and, really, her "sins" were so small, they were almost charming. He had to show her that he was more generous, basically, than her own father . . . who was willing to send her money to bail her out of difficulties, to telegram her messages of encouragement and love, but never to visit her when she needed support. He was always flying around with Rockefeller, always in "classified" meetings in Albany or Washington. Yes, it was Murray's newer style (since the age of 45, when a bad bout of Asian flu had floored him) to be more generous than anyone else. Somehow, his good looks had vanished, the smile lines had become deep indentations that caught and retained shadows, especially when he was in the company of people he knew detested him . . . and his mock-athletic body now seemed to sag . . . but his generosity was real, his love was real. . . . He had to have her. Otherwise: what?

He didn't want to consider that.

Rumors about her money were absurd. He didn't want money. If he really wanted money he could have married Helena Smith-Brooke, who financed the *American Ends & Means Review*, and who had always favored him over her present husband, a California poet. Anyway, Murray knew, with a certainty that could not be mistaken, that he would never benefit from Rosalind's fortune. It was just not Murray Licht's fate to be financially secure, but always to be broke, in debt, driven across the United States each spring and fall, reading his work anywhere they would have him. He needed all the money he could get. He had several ex-wives, a number of children, so many bills, $2300 owed in back taxes, not to mention the bewildering bill for $4000 for this year alone, from the child psychiatrist his 13-year-old went to three times a week . . . not to mention the terrible terms of his divorce settlement with Tanya, ages ago, when he'd been desperate to be free to marry pouty unpredictable Helga, alimony payments that would last as long as he existed. He knew Tanya wouldn't die first. He would never be financially secure, never. He would be a poet-in-residence somewhere, anywhere, teaching extra courses at night, surreptitiously, giving lectures or readings, he would do this forever, and forever would he sign up, each fall, each spring, for the larger of the poetry-reading circuits. Poets less financially desperate might sign on for the smallest circuits—the 4-stop or the 8-stop—but it was obviously Murray's special fate to be rotated around the 15-stop wheel. Actually, these circles criss-crossed one another, though a poet could opt generally for the "New England" or the "Midwest" or the "West"—the other circuits, like the "South," were sketchy and didn't pay as well; and there was some freedom of choice, though usually it was too tiring to attempt to figure out which route might be less exhausting. Yes, it was tiring even to think about these things. . . .

A knock at the door startled him: he'd better hang up. He snatched up the manila envelope and was about to shuffle the poems inside, then recalled that he had already done so. He was running ahead of schedule. Bobbie Sutter and Brian Fuller and a few students were in the hall, ready to escort him over to Ogg Center. "I'm usually a nervous wreck before a reading, but you look so composed," Bobbie Sutter said. As they strolled across the campus it seemed to have developed that Murray had actually napped, he had the power of sleeping and refreshing himself as, Sutter remarked, men like Lyndon Johnson and Winston Churchill had also had. "Just lay down somewhere and slept for ten minutes and woke up totally rejuvenated, while younger men around them staggered with exhaustion. . . . What a wonderful talent!" Sutter said. The others agreed. Brian Fuller said that if he had to give a reading on a strange campus, he'd be a nervous wreck, but Murray looked so composed. . . .

*   *   *   *

Murray was pleased at the turnout—at least 150, maybe 200 students, and a scattering of familiar faces—the younger faculty members, who now looked to him like very old friends, almost relatives, smiling enthusiastically at him. At first he was disappointed that Professor Stone was going to introduce him, but, though Stone did ramble slightly, and a few of the students looked

154

bored, his introduction was extremely flattering: he spoke at length about each of Murray's books, quoted from his favorite poem, enumerated the truly impressive list of Murray's awards and grants and the variety of publications he had published in ("from the *Times Literary Supplement* to the *Salty Dog Broadside*, and everywhere in between"), so that Murray's eyes filled with tears . . . such sincerity, such warmth, without a trace of irony! He wished that he might leave before Joachim Myer arrived, with his vicious good-natured cynicism and his superior knowledge of what was what, of who Murray Licht really was. . . . But this was marvelous, Professor Stone was a wonderful old man. If only Rosalind could hear him . . . !

He was met by generous applause from the audience and as soon as he began to read he forgot, as usual, whatever was troubling him. In a matter of seconds he actually became happy, or began to experience the symptoms of happiness. He could rely upon himself . . . he had taken voice lessons in New York City as a young man . . . and, a few years ago, after a reading in Miami (of Ohio) when he had run panicked out of the hall, he had taken a form of behavioral therapy called desensitization, which had benefited him enormously. His terror had become toned down to the point at which it might be mistaken for simple excitement or enthusiasm. Though Murray's poetry was really quite difficult, finely-crafted, and allusive, he was able to compensate for this by modulating his voice dramatically. Despite the high intellectual content of most of his work, audiences rarely became restless and not too many left early.

. . . For the first fifteen minutes he read love poems, tenderly and yet wittily; then, sensing the need for a change, he switched to the brusque, brutal mock-"colloquial" sonnets he'd tried in the Sixties; then, sensing that antiwar sentiment was dated, he switched to the poems in his first book, *Festered Lilies*, and concluded with the title poem, which was long and elegiac, in the style of Wallace Stevens, a quite nihilistic work which always seemed, at least to college audiences, to be somehow positive and "nature-worshipful." So he ended the reading after fifty-five minutes, to generous applause. Yes, it really was generous: he was awfully grateful.

He thanked them all.

He hoped, now, to be driven back to the Inn, but people swarmed around him—students and faculty wives—requesting autographs in his books or on slips of paper—Bobbie and Brian and Sandy and Professor Stone and a few others were congratulating him, shaking hands, remarking that it went very well—he saw Bobbie draw his hand across his forehead in a gesture of relief—what did that mean?—and a freckled bouncy woman insisted upon taking him aside, introducing herself as Caroline Metzner, didn't he remember her?—he must remember her—she thought he had done magnificently, he was truly a genius, and how lucky he was that crotchety old demon Tim Lyndon had stayed away—Orbach had nearly been reduced to tears the day before and, she said, passionately, "it's just tragic to see a man cry, even an undersized man like Orbach."

"Undersized?" Murray asked. Orbach had not been undersized in the past. . . . But now Sutter and Fuller came to his rescue, escorting him out of the Center, while Caroline Metzner and a few others trailed along. There was a chorus of *Didn't it go over well!* and *Didn't he go over well!* and, at Fuller's station wagon, Caroline Metzner asked if she could ride with them to the Inn, linking her arm through Murray's. Murray signalled Fuller *no, dear God, no!* but he seemed not to understand, and they all piled into the station wagon. At the Inn, however, Murray was able to make the woman realize that he was already late for another appointment, he just couldn't see her right now, and she smirked cheerfully and said she'd been good enough for him three years ago at Athens, Ohio, but she supposed times changed. . . . Murray told her that he had never been in Athens, Ohio, which was the truth as far as he could recall.

"Back at six sharp," Fuller announced.

Murray staggered into the Inn, through the lobby, like a man in a dream—dazed, jarred—yet somehow able to recognize this place, to remember that his room was in a certain direction; as if he'd been staying at the Lapointe Inn for weeks. He made his way unerringly to his room. Inside, he tried to summon up the joy he'd felt as he heard that applause . . . real, genuine, unironic applause . . . but it was marred somewhat by his knowledge that Rosalind would never be able to exactly imagine it. . . . Then someone knocked at the door. He had the option of not answering, but for some perverse reason he answered it: it was Harmon Orbach.

*   *   *   *

"How did it go?—your reading?" Orbach asked at once.

Murray stared at him. How his old friend had changed!— though he was four years younger than Murray he looked shrunken, almost shrivelled, his skin pale, egg-shell-pale, most of his hair thinned away, his eyes smaller and meaner than Murray remembered. There had been rumors about Orbach taking drugs, but Murray had never believed them. Now, there was a stark, staring, maliciously vacuous look to him that was really alarming. Murray stammered a reply, saying it had gone fairly well, since he didn't want to boast of his success and he knew Orbach had hoped to hear bad news. Orbach asked him whether some old guy, he forgot the name, whether this old son of a bitch was on hand?—asking about yahoos?—or making the noise "yahoo," whatever the word meant? —but Murray pretended to know nothing about this, nothing at all. "Why, did he bother you?" he asked.

"Forget it," Orbach said.

He made himself at home, collapsing into the room's only chair, extending his legs, sighing, wheezing, muttering. Murray tried not to keep staring at him. Both men were wearing the same outfit— an unfortunate coincidence, but who could have foreseen it?— black trousers, a black pull-over jersey shirt, and a leather belt. Murray's belt was black, however, and Orbach's was brown. It clashed with his outfit, cut his figure in half and seemed to make him look even smaller. Orbach sat for a while with his eyes closed, as if this were his room and he were alone, then he opened them sharply and asked what the hell time it was. ". . . there's a banquet somewhere at 6:15 . . . and that gangster Myer is giving a talk at 8 . . . then a panel of all of us . . . then a party. . . . Then I'm done

1 5 7

till Monday morning," he said. "I'm due out at Erie Tech, you ever been there?"

"Pittsburgh?"

"No, Duluth."

"I might have been there, years ago," Murray said. There was nothing to do but offer Orbach a drink, since he was going to have one himself. Orbach accepted the drink gratefully; he even smiled. His mouth moved normally. Murray wanted to ask about the "panel"—he hadn't quite realized that he would be on a panel that evening—or had he forgotten it?—and he doubted whether he could endure a party afterward. But he didn't want to show Orbach any signs of weakness. He spoke enthusiastically about the Lapointe people; the students were lively and well-read, especially for Iowa; and the luncheon had been most enjoyable, too bad Orbach hadn't showed up.

Orbach made a sniggering noise. The drink was having a visible effect on him—he already looked less drained, more now like a puckered leprechaun than a malicious dwarf. "How come you suddenly started avoiding me?" he asked Murray. "We got along so well that summer—you and some girl who was typing for you—remember?—Christ, you practically thrived out there, on my farm —Kentucky, remember?—outside Lexington, remember? You got to looking real healthy, instead of washed-out and sickly, like you do now . . . it must be the basic New York look, the way you are now."

"I don't think I ever visited your farm," Murray said slowly. "No, I'm sure I never did. I stayed with Richie James and his girl friend and two of his kids . . . but it wasn't in Kentucky, I think it was in Florida. . . ."

"Murray Licht and a girl, a blonde, getting her M.A. at Radcliffe," Orbach said. He wagged his finger. "Marilyn never knew a damn!"

"I don't think that was me," Murray said. But he was not certain—vaguely, he did remember Orbach in connection with faulty plumbing and a lot of large black flies. "I know you have a farm in Kentucky, Harmon, but—"

"Past tense," he said. "Had to be sold. . . . I'm $5000 in debt," he said conversationally. "I'm living now in Chicago, teaching at the Circle, renting an unbelievable dump for $250 a month . . . but the hell with it . . . what do you care, eh, engaged to a steel Muse?. . . . The point is . . . the point is. . . ."

But he had lost the point.

Murray poured more Scotch into their glasses.

". . . the point is, Murray, that the Dominic freak is getting $800 for this and I'm getting only $400. I discovered that yesterday. I saw some Xeroxed paper that bastard Bobbie Sutter had in his office."

"$400?" Murray asked.

He was getting only $300, himself.

"And get this, Murray, that son of a bitch Myer, that actual criminal, who charges were almost brought against for how he handled the cash backing the, what was it, Academy of Arts and Letters, or something, that guy is getting $1000! For one fifty-minute lecture! He's flying in as late as possible and they have to drive 100 miles to Des Moines to get him—then they're rushing him back here like a hero—and *he* gets to skip the classes and the banquet and just makes some special endowed lecture—collects his check and clears out—how the hell do you like that?"

Murray muttered something.

"Hannah Dominic has been hanging around here since Tuesday," Orbach said. ". . . poisoning people against me, against both of us . . . you know why? Because we're men! Masculine! . . . a loud-mouthed maniac, no closer to being a poet than . . . than . . . Joachim Myer. Last night there was a shouting match at somebody's house, some nice pathetic couple that had a dinner party in my honor, Hannah said she was degraded by sharing the bill with you and me . . . said your poetry was reactionary crap. Mine wasn't much better, she said, but I'm too much of a degenerate to be a threat, and a few people at the party actually laughed. . . . Some of these faculty wives, they *laugh* at things."

"No one told me about all this," Murray said, depressed.

"Yeh. She was feeling great because of the huge crowd she got.

She was scheduled for Ogg Center, but so many kids showed up they had to move the reading to the Science Building, where there's an auditorium like an arena. She can't read right, her poetry is lousy, so she shouts a lot—swings her arms. They seemed to like her." Orbach finished his drink. "I wish she would die."

Murray pretended not to have heard this.

". . . one poem she read, it was dedicated to you," Orbach said, smiling. "Crazy nasty thing, sort of funny, called 'Pig-Castrating' . . . the kids just loved it. You know, Hannah is really serious, she means every bit of it. They all do."

"Who?"

"Women."

So in Harmon he discovered an ally.

They chatted for a while about how things were going. Harmon complained bitterly about the money he had wasted on a trip to Japan, he craved Zen enlightenment more than anything in the world, literally hungered for it!—but when he arrived at the monastery at Ryutaku, where it had supposedly been arranged for him to stay, the roshi had refused him admittance—the Jap bastard —some excuse about them being filled up with Americans, and Harmon hadn't looked "in good health" or some such prejudiced excuse—"and those people claim, they actually claim, to be compassionate," Harmon said. Murray shook his head sympathetically. He, the grandson of a rabbi, descended from impoverished but very pious men, knew that it was probably part of his destiny to be deeply and crazily religious—but it would have cost him what little of his reputation remained, in New York City, at least, and anyway he had no idea how to go about it. Ascent of the soul? *Aliyath han'shamah?* It would have been impossible to work anything like that, anything so cumbersome, into his elegant poetry. . . . no, better stay with what was immediate.

Harmon continued, as if reading Murray's mind, saying that the Zen failure had catapulted him back into reality: nice gross physical real reality. "I really thought this one might be, you know, intellectual and ethereal . . . I don't mean physically, because she isn't an attractive woman that way . . . in fact quite homely. . . .

But the *conversation*, I thought! So I became involved with . . ." and here he mentioned a name that made Murray sit up, since this lady critic, notorious for her lengthy, vicious, wrong-headed but somehow irrefutable reviews, had once praised Murray Licht . . . for all the wrong reasons, of course, but Murray had certainly been pleased. He detested women like her: sour, leaden, witty and wordy, so unlike Rosalind they might have come from another planet. Yet it was usually these women who admired his poetry, while Rosalind loved *The Prophet* and was still attached to J. D. Salinger.

"It was doomed from the start," Harmon said thickly. "The old bag is twenty years past her prime, panting and puffing and bulging all over, so stingy she actually questioned me, one day, about some grapes . . . it turned out her kid had eaten them. Everybody thinks she has these high standards, to judge from her reviews, and it turns out she just hates everybody . . . even me, now. When I walked out she screamed and threatened suicide, then threatened to ask for my books to review, for the *Times*, but I had to escape . . . though I haven't been able to write a line since. . . . Oh God, Murray," he said. "How long will we be at it?"

He dozed off in the chair, so Murray was able to telephone Rosalind again. This time, the line was busy, which seemed to him encouraging—really, it was a good sign. It meant that she was actually in the apartment. In a perverse way Murray felt almost as if he had spoken to her. He felt almost cheerful. Certainly he was far better off than Harmon, whose wife had left him years before, and whose girls—the halfway attractive ones, that was—were always scruffy and diseased-looking, illiterates who would have been unable to appreciate the ten or twelve genuinely good poems Orbach had actually written, years ago.

But they were allies, after all, and rode together in Fuller's station wagon, back to the Ogg Center. Fuller came to pick them up at 6 sharp.

In the banquet hall they parted company—Orbach drifting off to sign a book held out to him by a tall, eager woman who seemed to have sideburns, Murray led over to Hannah Dominic, led almost forcibly by Brian Fuller, who introduced the two of them in a hearty good-natured voice. Hannah seemed too startled to draw away. She actually shook hands with Murray, caught off-guard. He was pleased to see how short she was, just a skinny famished ugly stringy-haired girl, probably intimidated by his size and superior reputation. He was slightly drunk, and so able to carry the awkward meeting off beautifully. "At last! I'm very honored to meet you at last!" he said. Several girl students lingered nearby, listening closely. But Hannah was too confused to say anything except *Thank you;* she had to keep shaking her head in order to get her hair out her eyes, a nervous mannerism that took up a lot of her time. So Murray took advantage of her nervousness to say, loudly, that Lapointe College was certainly a lively place, wasn't it?—and the girls very pretty, weren't they?—and he could smell the odors of a fine banquet meal brewing, couldn't she?—and wasn't it an honor for the two of them to share equal billing with Harmon Orbach, one of the finest lyric poets in the country?

She muttered something in reply to this, but Murray went on to ask her about editors and poets and literary people they supposedly knew. He even escorted her to the head table—what bad luck, they were seated side by side!—chatting with her as if the two of them were not separated by more than a generation, as if they were really linked somehow and he didn't detest her and everything she stood for.

He helped her with her chair, a folding chair that hadn't been quite unfolded.

Once seated, however, Hannah regained her composure. She turned rudely away from him in order to talk to a woman on her left. Murray could hear her remarks quite plainly: ". . . the two of them drunk, just as I predicted . . ." ". . . Orbach is a coke-head, and *this* one, next to me . . . you can probably smell his breath over there." Murray kept his smile. Thank God, he was seated next to Professor Stone, who seemed too exhausted and oddly sad to bother to talk. A few seats down, Orbach was crammed in between Sandy Michaels and the boy, Scottie, who were both flush-faced and talkative, maybe a little drunk. His eyes caught at Murray's, wildly.

Murray just smiled, one soul in hell smiling at another; look who *he* was seated next to.

Hannah's sharp angry voice seemed to dwindle. As the first course was served—shrimp cocktail, two tiny tightly-bent shrimp pierced by a tiny green plastic sword, and a lot of seafood sauce splashed on some lettuce—Murray actually thought he might be going deaf, seriously. It would not surprise him. Though this spring reading tour had begun only 9 days ago, it seemed that he had been on it forever . . . steadily degenerating, forever . . . he and the other poets of the spring circuits rotating around one another, circling one another endlessly, in orbit, in widening and narrowing and intersecting circles . . . carried now by their own momentum, by the remorseless laws of nature themselves, which had nothing to do with a human invention called "poetry." They encountered one another, sat down beside one another the way he and "Hannah Dominic" were together, right now, then moved on, helplessly, hopelessly, growing older, shabbier, more and more in debt. . . . It was unfortunate, the fact that the men poets far outnumbered the women. Aside from Hannah, who flew everywhere to give readings, there were only two or three women on the circuit . . . the rest were too shy, or too unstable, or too incompetent. The women poets of Murray's generation had rarely gone out into the field; they had been gracious, real ladies . . . not competitors at all. Though Hannah's toga-like outfit with the baggy droopy sleeves did remind Murray of a woman poet he had admired, ages ago . . . now dead. Deceased. Immortalized. Safe.

The appetizer was taken away and salad brought, in shallow, shiny wooden dishes. Hannah turned abruptly back to Murray, though not to talk to *him*; instead she called irritably down the length of the table to Bobbie Sutter, asking him if her room had been changed yet—evidently she'd been awakened two mornings in a row by air-hammer noises, from the construction work—and Bobbie smiled and seemed to be saying *Yes*, though it really wasn't clear. He then looked away, since a student waiter was asking him a question. "Did you know the student union can't serve drinks?— notice, no drinks?" Hannah said to Murray. At first he thought she

163

might be taunting him, but evidently she was trying to be friendly. She seemed to swerve from side to side, restless, nervous, angular, pointy, her elbow colliding with Murray's, and her long swooping sleeve brushing into his salad. Her toga was made of a coarse black material, almost as heavy as canvas.

Now the banquet began in earnest. Each heavy white plate contained a slab of roast beef, and mashed potatoes, across which had been spooned some still-warm dark gravy. A side dish of corn-and-carrot mix, which Murray recognized because it resembled the pictures on frozen food containers; and Parker House rolls; and a single pat of butter on its tiny white cardboard square, protected by a tiny white square of tissue. Murray could not distinguish between the different things on his plate, except by their texture, by how much effort it cost him to chew. Midway through the meal Hannah pushed her plate away and lit a cigarette. She poked Murray and chuckled, "I know a secret!—something you don't know!" He stared at her. Her pale, plain face was brought up close to his. It was so real, somehow—so uncontrived, so raw and bald a face, not only unbeautiful but unrelated to beauty—possessing a power that terrified him, because it had nothing to do with him at all. He thought of Rosalind's soft, fair skin, the delicate arc of her eyebrows—surely she and Hannah Dominic did not belong to the same sex—and horribly, as if in a dream, Hannah seemed to know exactly what he was thinking. She said: "The one you're marrying next, eh? Rosalind, eh? *Very* pretty—ravishing! I knew her at Bennington." Murray drew back in horror. "Not as well as some knew her, of course—"

Fortunately their conversation was interrupted by an announcement that Joachim Myer had arrived on campus, "everyone will be pleased to know," and that his lecture would be given as planned, at 8 P.M. sharp, so they must hurry the final part of the banquet: the awards ceremony. Bobbie Sutter was speaking in the same sunny hearty voice Murray had been greeted with, that morning, so long ago that he could barely recall it. Hannah leaned toward him to whisper something, but he put a finger to his lips, quieting her—how he dreaded this awful woman, who smirked at him know-

ingly!—Bobbie Sutter read off the list of the student winners of
the poetry contest, beginning with the pseudonym "Shake S.
Peare," which caused appreciative titters, followed by applause as
the real names were given; there was a great deal of confusion
afterward, as three or four students crowded around Murray,
thanking him, one of them the long-haired boy, shaking his hand
and thanking him emotionally, almost passionately. "Mr. Licht,
this means so much to me . . . I don't know, it sort of changes my
life . . . I, uh, don't want to make any goddam scene or anything,"
the boy said, his eyes glittering madly, "but, uh . . . well OK . . . I
better get out of here." And he rushed away, his head lowered.

So the banquet ended.

It was five minutes to eight. They mustn't linger, since it was
quite a hike across campus to the Science Building; Murray was
herded along with Hannah Dominic, under Brian Fuller's black
umbrella—it had started to rain, quite hard—and Harmon Orbach
was just ahead of them, squeezed in between Sandy Michaels and
Scottie, who both had umbrellas. There was a great deal of chatter
and excitement, though Murray was too dazed to pay much attention. He and Hannah kept bumping into each other. Neither seemed
to notice, though, and Hannah spent most of the walk trying to light
a cigarette, but, since she had to keep going, pressed forward by
Brian Fuller's arm, she was never able to get it lit. Murray knew
there was something Hannah had almost told him—but he could
not remember it, for some reason—was he losing his mind?—but
Hannah herself seemed to have forgotten. Murray felt a pang of
jealousy when he saw, up ahead, how Sandy Michaels had slipped
her arm through Harmon's. She *liked* Harmon Orbach. Obviously,
she preferred him to Murray himself. He felt so tired, so perplexed
. . . he so dreaded the next part of the evening, having to endure
Joachim Myer . . . having to share a stage with him, simply to
admit that Myer existed . . . he found himself staring past the edge
of the umbrella at the early evening sky, the dark, deep-glowing
blue banks of clouds, and thinking of how, one day, his mind might
sail up into that wordless beauty: into a future that already existed,
that had existed from the beginning of history. *And would they*

marry, after all? Or would she escape?—for one woman, obviously, would escape him.

*   *   *   *

The auditorium on the first floor of the Science Building was already jammed—noisy and much too brightly-lit—Murray and the others had to make their way down the crowded steps, where students were sitting, excusing themselves, apologizing, fearful of being knocked over. This place was far too brightly-lit, Murray thought; he was accustomed to auditoriums with softer lights. On stage was a long table with a speaker's podium in the center and for the first time Murray realized that he would really be forced to sit through a "lecture" by Joachim Myer. . . . As an undergraduate at Columbia, Myer had been skinny, a hypochondriac, obsessed with the need to make others acknowledge his genius . . . Murray's only serious rival . . . they invariably found themselves enrolled in the same courses, competing frantically and mercilessly with each other: ultimately, Murray supposed that *he* had won. His grade point average was slightly higher. And, though Myer did publish a well-received book of poems, at the age of twenty-four, he, Murray, had published a better-received book of poems, at the age of twenty-six; and that book, *Festered Lilies*, had been a contender for the National Book Awards. And so. . . . But he was forced out of his muttered reverie by someone giving him instructions. Sit here, here, Mr. Licht, yes fine. He sat. Hannah Dominic blundered into the folding chair beside him, but was told that her place was on the other side of the speaker's podium—over there, yes fine—and someone led her away. Murray sipped at the glass of water he found before him. He was very nervous, but why? . . . this would be over soon and in the morning he'd fly to Mobridge, South Dakota. Perhaps Kitimit, Iowa, had been only a dream.

Students were still pushing into the auditorium, though all the seats were taken. Many were sitting on the stars; others were standing back against the wall; a dozen or more had been given permission to sit up on stage, back near the exits, provided they did not

166

cause any commotion. It was quite noisy. Murray noticed Brian Fuller on his left and Harmon Orbach on his right; at the other end of the table Hannah was flanked by Bobbie Sutter and a man Murray couldn't remember, who was evidently the moderator. Joachim Myer was in the wings, strolling in this direction, chatting with admiring students—there he was, Myer himself—Murray couldn't help but stare at him. It must be admitted that Joachim looked good. He wore a stylish outfit, dark green trousers and a lemon-green jacket, a white silkish shirt, and a broad yellow necktie that had the texture of raw silk. He was guffawing about something, shaking his head, and Murray was struck by his tan, his confidence, his thick gray-black hair. He and Myer were about the same age, yet no one would have guessed it. For a while, in their twenties, they had looked equally young; then Murray had begun pulling away from Joachim, having the appearance at first of being five years older . . . then, maybe, eight years older. . . . For a while he had looked a decade older than Joachim but now, tonight, he had to admit that most members of the audience would have guessed at least twenty years difference. Joachim saw him, smiled, waved in a most friendly but unenthusiastic way, and Murray made a noncommital gesture in return. Where were Joachim's glasses? His eyes gleamed, almost glinted; he must be wearing contact lenses.

And now the introduction: given by a dapper, dramatic professor of Communication Arts, whom the students seemed to like. They laughed at remarks Murray had not known were meant to be funny. It was depressing to have to sit through a lengthy description of Joachim's career . . . especially when it stressed only the public positions and grants and editorships and awards . . . while *he*, Murray, knew the inside story. It was true that Joachim had begun as a poet, a young man of wonderful promise, sensitive, brilliant, in the tradition of . . . and, yes, it was true that he had been awarded a Guggenheim . . . and . . . yes, all these facts were true, Murray wanted to shout, but what about Myer's nervous breakdown, his disappearance for several years, his inability to write any more poetry? . . . his *failure* as a poet? He had lived for a while in

Spain, on translations and hand-outs. Everyone had thought him finished, had written him off at the age of 35. Murray had certainly written him off. Hearing so many awful things about his old friend, his old rival, Murray almost come to sympathize with him; almost, he wished Joachim Myer had "lived up to his early promise."

Then something extraordinary happened. Myer published an essay in the *New York Review of Books* that dealt in an elliptical, witty manner with issues raised by Marshall McLuhan and George Steiner and Wittgenstein; a masterpiece of criticism, sheer style, though Murray was certainly baffled over what it meant. No one seemed to know exactly what it meant. But within a year Joachim was offered a professorship at Harvard, received another Guggenheim to help him complete his research, and began that steady ascendence that so amazed and intimidated everyone else. . . .

The applause finally died away.

"*What Was Poetry?*" Joachim began. He had a rather strident voice, but at least it carried well. Murray watched him covertly and saw the stack of notes—the speech was totally planned but Joachim was giving the impression of being spontaneous. He spoke so confidently and without hesitation that it took some effort to realize, as Murray did, that everything he said was absurd; it was nonsense; it was worse than Hannah Dominic's poetry. . . . Swift confusing references to Claude Lévi-Strauss and Buckminster Fuller . . . word-plays on terms from quantum physics . . . a dizzying equation of the statistics involving astrologers and astronomers (the former outnumbering the latter 40-1 at the present time) with the statistics involving the relationship of viewers of afternoon television soap operas, surf-board enthusiasts on the West Coast, and the square yardage of the United States that was under pavement. Murray glanced out at the audience, expecting to see derision or restlessness; but everyone was entranced. And yet— what garbage! Of course it was garbage! Was the world mad? *What was poetry? Why did it die? Who killed it? Why?* Electronic group-world. Group-think. Grope-think. Americanization of the cosmos. Manifest destiny: inner/outer space. Moonshot, inscape. Sunspots, outscape. Acid. Proud illiterates. Land of the free: freedom from tyranny of the Word. Venereal disease. Democratic vistas. The death of poetry. *Death! Death of the Word! Death of the Image! Death of the Void! Death of Death!*

"If the act be not ordained with its imperishable word-image, how shall it be experienced?" Joachim asked. "I bring you freedom! total liberation! the flood of the polymorphous-perverse cosmos denied you by your parents and by our arch-oppressor, Poetry!"

A round of applause. Joachim waited until it died away, then continued with a stream of cheerful rhythmic sounds that barely translated themselves into words—Murray wondered if he was losing the ability to think, he felt so confused by Joachim's flashing manner—freedom from tyranny, end of art, end of ego-consciousness, fascistic evil, end of "higher" education, end of "higher," rise of "lower," replacement, re-evaluation, rethink, rework, rerun, X-out Shakespeare substitute Russ Meyer, All Power to the People, populism, popular, pop. Civilization went into a spin, Joachim argued, with the invention of the printing press; but had begun its long hideous decline with the acceptance of the Word. "In the beginning was the Word," Joachim cried, "and the Word was of the Devil! And we are paying for it still—tonight—tonight especially —struggling not to suffocate beneath the oppression of ego-consciousness—"

He was so passionate, so convincing, that he was interrupted with more applause. Murray tried not to listen, he had heard enough . . . it alarmed him, though, to see so many rapt faces in the audience. Evidently the students liked Joachim. They believed him. They believed anything . . . anything . . . Murray glanced at Brian Fuller, who was sucking at an unlit pipe. Fuller was uneasy, as if he were only now beginning to understand Joachim's message. *What was poetry? What was consciousness?* Harmon Orbach moved restlessly, crossing and uncrossing his legs. At times he seemed about to interrupt Joachim, then hesitated. He was probably afraid. Bluish veins on the backs of his hands seemed to be throbbing, visibly. Dead? Were they all dead? *And why is it a good thing, a delightful thing?*—Joachim wanted to know. *Why, when the written word is killed, does the polymorphous-perverse body experience its resurrection?* Murray leaned back to see how Hannah Dominic was taking all this. She was whitefaced, incredulous. She was staring at Joachim with none of the sweetly-vicious hatred she'd lavished on Murray: this was sheer hate. In a ringing voice Joachim was concluding his talk with sweeping strings of words, puns, jokes, befuddlements, ending with the injunction that poetry in the post-acid culture must be only physical, each human being a poet with his body, a pop-artist of his body, having blotted out his evil consciousness forever.

"Forever and ever, Amen," Joachim said.

Vast waves of applause.

And more applause.

After so much excitement, it seemed something of an anti-climax when the moderator asked the panelists to comment, if they cared to. For a while no one spoke. Then Murray attempted a kind of rebuttal, but he heard his voice echoing through the microphone, feeble, meager, too defensive, not powerful enough to prevent a dozen or more people from leaving the auditorium. ". . . poetry has always had enemies . . . the voice of unreason . . . nazism . . . the lunatics among us, dressed in stylish suits . . . sucking up to the retarded of the nation . . ." It went over poorly. Harmon was asked to comment next, and, after a painful silence, he began to shout: "I want to go home! I want my farm! I want my babies back—my family! I want my poetry, my poetry—I—I want—" Students on their way out paused, to listen to Harmon's cries; the big auditorium was oddly silent except for a few scattered giggles. Murray happened to notice that woman, Caroline Metzner, maybe ten rows from the front, both hands pressed against her face in an attitude of exquisite scandalized delight. But the moderator acted quickly, thanking Harmon for his contribution, and now for Miss Dominic—would she comment, please?

She grabbed the microphone and panted into it. At first she could not even speak, then she cried out something about chauvinism in a new form—male repression—savagery—fascism— She was very upset; she seemed about to burst into tears. "—now that women are gaining control of their consciousnesses—their freedom—will—freedom of will—liberated from oppression—now—now that a new generation of women poets—a break-through in history—evil men like Joachim Myer want to annihilate everything—once again— It's a plot—a plot—"

Joachim evidently made a comic face of some kind, since the audience laughed. This confused Hannah; she stopped speaking.

"Please continue, Miss Dominic," the moderator said nervously.

Murray looked over at her. It was pitiful, the way she was hunched over the microphone, cringing there, one long floppy sleeve fallen back to her elbow to reveal a tense, freckled arm. Finally she shook her head and whispered that she hadn't anything more to say. The moderator was so confused himself that he forgot to call upon Bobbie Sutter, who was on the panel as Lapointe's poet-in-residence; he turned the microphone back over to Joachim Myer for "a few concluding remarks." How would Mr. Myer reply to these rebuttals?

Joachim hesitated, pretending to be thinking. He gave the impression of being "grave," as if the quality of these rebuttals had been so poor, so contemptible, that even to acknowledge them was difficult. In his lemon-green sports jacket, with his handsome silk tie and his tanned, healthy face, he looked like a tourist who has strayed into the wrong quarter; a man who must not breathe too deeply for fear of smelling something unpleasant. Then he said, wryly, that Mr. Harmon was "not quite so incoherent as his poetry," but incomprehensible just the same; this was met with loud appreciative guffaws, even from some of the faculty wives in the first several rows. And Hannah Dominic bore out, in his opinion, in her strangely defensive, illogical reply, "the very suppositions she and other so-called 'liberated' women attack: the incontestable terror and guilt women experience over having been castrated at birth, before birth, actually, which Freud recognized and attempted to explain, in his typically rational, systematic way, but which Miss Dominic hysterically denies . . . hence she has no choice but to project outward her legitimate terror over her loss, and she imagines that men like myself are attacking her . . . you see how contra naturam it is, for a woman to allow her *imagination* the freedom men can allow theirs!"

Hannah seized a microphone and began shouting, incoherently —Murray thought he heard *Pig! Stop! Don't let him! Kill him! Help me!*—then she burst into tears and ran off-stage, to a malicious scattering of applause. Joachim continued speaking as if nothing at all had happened; he was remarkably composed, as if encouraged by everyone else's deterioration. ". . . in fact it is men like myself who are working to liberate hysterical women, and men, also, by freeing them from all sexual roles, *all* sexual differentiations entirely . . . in fact, all differentiations of every type . . . so that we may return to the polymorphous joys of infancy . . . to the embrace of the Uruboros . . . our mother . . . And now, how shall I reply to Mr. Licht's remarks?" He paused, turning pointedly in Murray's direction. Yes, he was wearing contact lenses; Murray could see tiny glassy dots in his eyes, which caught and reflected the light. "Some of you may know that Murray Licht and I are old friends. Yes, old friends. But Murray fears me, for some reason . . . Murray and his kind fear me . . . though I want only to liberate them. How strange it is, how unnatural! . . . People like Murray Licht, symptoms of bourgeois decay . . . old ex-Marxists, tired liberals, not-quite-liberal liberals, cranky and sour and ulcerous with envy . . . of the primordial strengths represented by America, by the Federal Government, by liberators like myself . . . just plain envious! . . . People like Murray Licht are sick with envy, eaten with jealousy, over the synthesis of ideals represented by men like myself, Joachim Myer. Look at him squirming there! Look! He fears me because I represent the synthesis of the old ideals of success and the very latest, hardly-articulated ideals of success . . . the total triumph of the Id. . . . My relations with Murray, as with the New York-Boston crowd of so-called intellectuals, began to deteriorate precisely at that point in my personal life when I started to become happy—healthy—sane—and, yes, let me say it, let me say that forbidden word—*popular*. Now I've said it, eh, Murray? How they hate, how they translate their simple child-like envy into hatred, and that hatred into 'objective criticism'! But I see through

172

them all. And it gives me great delight to announce that, after I complete my spring lecture tour, I will be taking over the editorship—not an associate editorship, but *the* editorship—of a famous men's magazine—it would be immodest of me to mention its title—a magazine unashamedly dedicated to the pursuit of the polymorphous-perverse ideal!—though, of course, temporarily disguised as a conventional *men's* magazine. . . . But to return to Mr. Licht who, I may speculate, will *never* edit such a magazine, or be published in it, who might even feel justifiably depressed by glancing through it at a newsstand: I do honor the poetry of Murray Licht, in spite of what I've said. I respect it. It is 'high art,' it is finely-crafted—though no more finely-crafted than Meyer's classic film "Vixen"!—I acknowledge Mr. Licht's genius—his rightful place as one of America's most famous élitist poets, at least at the present time— But: I do not read Mr. Licht's work. And I hardly imagine that anyone in the audience reads it, just as none of us read *Euphues*, for instance, or Wallace Stevens. And if any of you do read it—haven't you anything more exciting to do?" Here, much laughter; applause. The Metzner woman was rocking from side to side, her cheeks bunched up with delight. "Mr. Licht insults me by suggesting that I cater to the retarded of the nation . . . failing to realize that the future belongs not to him but . . . to the retarded! Yes! To the retarded! Certainly! Murray Licht may protest and pout all he wants, but he can't stop history—not only might Licht be headed for oblivion, he might already—now—tonight—this instant—be extinct. Let's consider him as the last, the very last, of the famous poets . . . Well-crafted, witty, profound, intelligent, Eliot and Yeats and Stevens and all that oppressive crowd . . . impossible for them to compete with the moon-shot and the soap operas and the late late movies. . . . Impossible. Let there be no more poets."

Murray gaped at him. He had not heard most of this; but he had heard the word *famous*.

The program ended abruptly, because Joachim Myer had to leave. Murray realized he should say something further to defend poetry . . . it was evident that Harmon Orbach would not, nor was

Bobbie Sutter about to attempt a reply. . . . But somehow he let the opportunity pass, he was so strangely tired, annihilated and yet excited . . . hearing again and again that word *famous.* Had it really happened, or was he imagining it? Joachim Myer had flown all the way to Kitimit, Iowa, to say, before a huge crowd of rapt, admiring students, that *Murray Licht was a famous poet . . .? And a genius?*

How he wished Rosalind had heard it!

He had sometimes believed he was a genius, or had been at one time; everyone knew he was highly competent as a poet; intelligent, tasteful, a fine craftsman. . . . But *famous?* Had he been famous all this time, without knowing it?

Famous?

Joachim had to leave immediately; he was due in London the day after next—he had been asked to give the William Makepeace Thackeray Memorial Lecture at the University of London. "The same topic," he said in reply to someone's query. He shook hands with Murray, rather warmly. "Not bad, eh? The turnout here?" He winked at Murray, but Murray didn't understand what the joke was. "I'd give myself only a B—, I lack the spontaneity I used to have on this particular subject," Joachin said cheerfully, "but that Dominic bitch was certainly a success—almost stole the show— Well, Murray, I must be off, sorry we can't get together for a drink, but you're probably tied up too, eh?—and leaving in the morning for where?" Murray mumbled a reply, Joachim obviously couldn't have heard it, he was backing away, smiling, nodding, waving goodbye to everyone as if Murray and Harmon and the others had somehow participated with Joachim in a performance of some kind, and their annihilation was nothing serious. A joke, maybe. Joachim was in excellent spirits, a conqueror; he joined the drained, deathly-pale Bobbie Sutter, who was waiting to drive him 100 miles back to the Des Moines airport, waving goodbye senti-mentally. "Lots of fun, eh? Well— Tomorrow England—fresh woods, and pastures new!"

*   *   *   *

The three poets were driven back to the Lapointe Inn, by Brian Fuller. Evidently a reception had been planned following the Myer lecture, but it was cancelled for some reason. Fuller explained, evasively, that the Dean's wife, who had planned the reception, wasn't feeling well. . . . Then he said bitterly, "He promised he would stay for a reception . . . for an interview with the *Herald* . . . then he claimed not to remember. Well. I suppose a man like that, internationally famous, in constant demand. . . ."

Murray picked up the word *famous*. In spite of the shambles of the evening he couldn't help but feel cheerful; so it was a surprise to discover how really upset Orbach and Hannah Orbach were. Fuller let them out at the door, and they trudged through the lobby and upstairs toward their rooms, Hannah sobbing, saying this had been the worse night of her life, such humiliation, such agony. . . . Why, she was really crying! Harmon invited them all to his room. "Let's celebrate getting out of this place," he said thickly. ". . . celebrate the end of Iowa Poetry Week." Harmon too had been shaken, but he was reviving. In fact, it was extraordinary, the way that man could change: for a while, after his outburst, he had seemed to sink into a psychotic state, almost a catatonic trance; now that the program was over, now that they were by themselves, he sounded almost normal.

Murray hesitated joining them, since he wanted to place another call to Rosalind. However, it was 10:30 here in Iowa; it would be much later in New York. Perhaps it would be better, more considerate of him, to wait until morning to call her. . . . *Joachim Myer spoke casually of me as famous!*

So he got his own bottle and joined them in Harmon's room. Hannah was sniffing, still crying; she looked years older than she'd looked at dinner; haggard, ghastly, yet somehow attractive, very feminine now as she sat on the edge of Harmon's bed. . . . Harmon was trying to cheer her up. Murray said it hadn't been so bad, really. Hannah said, "Oh that swinish bastard . . . that Nazi. . . . He destroyed me! . . . us! He came here and destroyed us!" That was true; but why dwell upon it? Harmon said it was pointless to be depressed all night. He had spent decades being depressed; he

175

was through with all that. Murray settled down with a drink, sighing, and told Hannah that things could be worse—for instance, he had once been driven out of a lecture hall at Buffalo, chased by students with billyclubs who were liberating the campus—"they drummed me out, literally—there was a drummer and a boy with a fife among them—" Harmon reminisced about the reading he'd given at Stanford, when half the English faculty walked out; it had been planned ahead of time, he insisted. Murray countered with incidents out of his vast tumultuous past; for he had known action everywhere, had known them all—the tiny girls' schools nestled in the hills, where he would read poems into shrill silence; the big land-grant universities of the Midwest, where he'd get lost on his way to the Alumni Center and his room, and end up walking for miles through agricultural complexes, cutting through pastures, weeping with frustration and sorrow; the big boxed-in city universities, like Wayne State, where his poetry reading in an exquisite glass building had been interrupted by gunshots, as Detroit police chased some Black Panthers across the quad, around back of the library, and shot them down in one of the faculty parking lots.

Hannah shuddered. But she seemed to feel a little better, and when Harmon Orbach offered them something in a white jar—cocaine, he said shyly, and the very best—she hesitated only a moment before accepting. She sniffed a pinch of it, delicately, in a stiff maidenish way. When Harmon laughed she said, blushing, "Oh please don't laugh!—not after what happened to me tonight!" Murray declined at first; he told Harmon that he was an alcoholic, and thought it best to stick with that. But Harmon insisted, so he gave in, he sat beside Hannah on the bed and took a few grains of the white powder, already feeling a high, weird, inexpressible calm—he liked Hannah after all, she was ugly, yes, and witchy, but she was a poet like himself, even a friend of Rosalind's, it seemed—and of course he had always liked Harmon Orbach, a very old friend. Harmon was saying excitedly that they must celebrate the end of poetry week!—the end of poetry!—the end of everything!

. . . Murray woke, not knowing where he was: fully-clothed, his shoes still on, lying sideways on a bed somewhere . . . in the company of Harmon Orbach and a woman with long stringy hair . . . both of them snoring and wheezing in utter abandonment, Orbach's arm flung across Murray's face. The woman turned out to be Hannah Dominic. Murray extricated himself from his friends and staggered over to the window. Two floors below was a swimming pool— its canvas covering weighed down with puddles of water in which birds frolicked in the morning sunshine—curious dark birds with streaks of red and yellow on their wings—robins, were they? Everything was sunny, glowing, utterly fresh. Murray did not know what had led to this, his standing here, blinking, staring—he felt razed, emptied, broken, beaten, annihilated—exhausted and defeated, yes, and yet so eerily, so involuntarily happy.

Famous . . . ?

ANGST

Just get the right syllable in
the proper place.
—Jonathan Swift

It was the worst of times—so she had been warned, and it should not have alarmed her to see so many intoxicated people—alcohol, drugs?—here in the elegant lobby of the Palmer House. But it was disconcerting. Bernadine, no more than five feet two, carrying her own small suitcase because the porters were so busy, got trapped in a *cul de sac* in the lobby, cut off by an enormous leather sofa at one end and a drunken group of young men at the other. They were all Midwestern, judging from their accents; one of them was being congratulated by the others, even jabbed playfully in the ribs, *An interview? How'd you swing it?* Bernadine excused herself, trying to get by. *Yeh, nine in the morning,* someone said. Then they noticed Bernadine and let her past.

Wiry, brusque, with an impatient and athletic little body, Bernadine had always been dismayed by her short stature and her small hands and feet. Most of the time she wore suits of a trim, tailored cut; but because she didn't want people to recognize her at the convention she had dressed in soft colors and fabrics, she even wore earrings, and her dull red hair was fluffed out around her face, instead of drawn back into a twist, as she usually wore it. Waiting in the crush of people by the elevators, she realized she had made a mistake. The agitation of being here—she half-knew she should not have come—was exaggerated by her costume, which did not represent her and which forced her to stand out, since the style this year among women professors and students was evidently quite mannish: most wore pants-suits, all wore outfits of dark neutral colors. Bernadine sensed herself far too feminine.

But the crowd was jammed in so tightly, and the mood so noisily festive, that none of the men seemed to notice her; they did not stand back to let her into the elevator. Only after several elevators were filled could she make her way in. Even so, a bearded man at least six foot three inches tall somehow stepped on her, and turned to mumble an apology into her face; his breath smelled of liquor. *Sorry. Didn't notice you.*

Up in her room she walked about, nervously, unable to sit down. She was waiting for Herman Geller's call. He had persuaded her to fly out to Chicago—he had "something urgent to beg of her." His letters always included references to "our common interests," "our future," but she did not dare to hope he really wanted to marry her. . . . And he had made the point, again and again, that it would be wise of her to meet with some of these academic people, especially those who were interested in her fiction. She would never meet them, of course: the very idea repulsed her, it was so vulgar. But she could not resist a kind of perverse curiosity. She paced around the room, leafing through the convention's bulky program notes until she came to the item that pertained to her—a panel of three, *The fiction of B. G. Donovan. 11 a.m. Cameo Room.*

When Herman did call, some forty-five minutes later, she snatched the phone up. "Herman, I'm afraid," she said.

"Be right up," he said at once.

He took her for drinks in the cocktail lounge, a kind of outdoor cafe in the lobby itself, though it was screened from the milling jabbering crowd by a mock-stone wall topped with artificial ivy. So much confusion!—but it helped to calm her, since no one would recognize her, obviously, and there was no need for her to feel self-conscious. She lived so quietly, so much to herself, that the very phenomenon of so many human beings—so much commotion, movement—actually soothed her, in a way, since it allowed her an anonymity that was precious. She dreaded attention, she loathed the very idea of being popular: she wrote with great care, labor-iously, in long hand, and then in numerous typed-out drafts . . . revisions, total rewritings . . . several times total rejections of novels she had spent many months creating. . . . *Sensitive. Exquisitely-wrought. Refined, utterly sane, "perfect."* These were the adjectives reviewers had given each of her five slender books. Until the recent year or so she had received no lengthier, more serious attention, and so it meant more to her than she was admitting to Herman—this seminar of "Donovan" specialists, this risky adventure of hers in Chicago.

"No, no! You shouldn't be apprehensive at all!" Herman said, squeezing her hand and releasing it. "You deserve the highest praise, the most meticulous attention . . . I've always told you, haven't I, it's been sixteen? . . . eighteen? . . . years now since I did that review of your first novel. . . . *One of those who maintain the Jamesian tradition . . . . valuable beyond our estimation. . . .* Didn't I say that? Certainly. And after dinner we'll go to the party I told you about, where I'll introduce you to certain people . . . friends of mine . . . I'm so grateful that you actually came here, Bernadine, it means so much to me. . . . I'm very proud to know you, very honored. . . . I must admit, I halfway expected you not to come!"

Now that they were together, their knees bumping beneath the small, inadequate table, Bernadine stared at Herman and wondered if perhaps it had been a mistake . . . she should not have left New York, she should not have been persuaded to take this step. He might ask her to marry him, again. He had asked her several times, in fact each time he came to New York City. He made the trip from Minnesota to New York three or four times a year, always visiting Bernadine, taking her out for dinner—yet it was always a surprise, she was never qiute prepared for the man's large, broad, slightly pitted face, the roundish expanse of his forehead, which seemed often to glow from within like a lamp. Now that he was balding this impression was stronger. His eyebrows were both tangled and scanty, the brown hairs wiry, curly, not lying flat against his face but pointing in all directions. His voice, too, was prepossessing, almost hypnotic. A small man, only an inch or so taller than Bernadine, he always seemed much taller. Perhaps it was because he changed his glasses—or at least the rims—several times a year that Bernadine was always disoriented. And he had begun to speak with a slight nasal tang. Originally from Boston, with advanced degrees from Harvard and Oxford, he had always told Bernadine how he loathed the Midwest; in recent years it seemed to be catching up with him.

While Herman talked, occasionally interrupting himself to call out to someone and wave, or to order another drink, Bernadine stared at the crowds in the lobby, fascinated. She had never attended one of these conventions before. Though she wrote critical essays occasionally, she had never taught in a university, and had of course never accepted any of the half-dozen offers of "writer-in-residence" that had come her way this past year. She was fiercely moral about her art: it must come first. She kept notebooks, journals, diaries of various kinds, simultaneously, and constantly wrote and rewrote and re-imagined her novels. She brought to literature the same ascetic, rather competitive professionalism certain of her relatives had brought to everything they did, back home in Virginia: horseback riding as well as community leadership and business. She had rejected their narrow interests, but did believe that their attitude toward life was correct; how could it not be correct, when it was so well-rewarded, so well-praised? She forbade herself to think at any length about the reviewers' enthusiastic judgments, yet at times their lavish adjectives flooded into her consciousness: *exquisite . . . sane . . . "perfect."*

The Palmer House was decorated for Christmas, but no one took notice. There was an enormous fir tree set up at the far end of the lobby, wired in place, but from where Bernadine sat it looked like something as artificial as the huge crystal chandeliers and the baroque gilded railings of the mezzanine balconies. Once inside, it was difficult to realize that the Chicago streets were windswept and frigid; tiny harsh bits of snow, not really snowflakes but sand-like bits, were driven along by winds so powerful that Bernadine had almost been knocked over, getting out of her taxi.

"It's almost pleasant here," Bernadine said suddenly. "Are all these people professors?"

"Some are students," Herman said. "A few of my graduate students are here, in fact . . . I hope I don't run into them, it's too pathetic. Another drink? No? We have plenty of time before dinner."

But Bernadine had just noticed someone, approaching them from the area near the elevators. A strangely-dressed woman . . . wearing what Bernadine believed was a poncho or a serape . . . yet it was over her shoulders like a cape; her dress was made of aged crushed velvet, a bright green . . . falling to mid-calf, too long and at the same time too short to be stylish. She walked slowly, too slowly. Her hair was uncombed, frizzy, almost woolly, a too-harsh red, obviously dyed, and her face was gaunt, white-powdered, far too serious. Bernadine felt a rush of pity for the woman—really a young woman in her thirties—and interrupted Herman to ask, "Who is she?—there? Do you see that poor young woman over there?"

Herman adjusted his glasses and peered over at her. She was now approaching a small group of people, men and two young women, and Bernadine saw how they stared at her, their smiles strained, frightened. . . . The red-haired woman wore desert boots, and the expanse of leg Bernadine could see was too-white and reddened on its surface, as if scraped. And the awful crushed velvet dress . . . and the coarse oatmeal-colored poncho . . . and the gestures her hands made, now too slow, now too jerky. . . . Several rings on her fingers, and pendulum-like earrings, gypsy earrings. And. . . .

Herman had been telling Bernadine about an interview he hoped to have with Robert Lowell next spring, a television-taped interview sponsored by an educational network; it was with an irritable expression that he said, "Oh yes. Her. . . . But she's harmless."

"Do you know her?" Bernadine asked, surprised.

"Max Lippe was her advisor at Berkeley, I believe; do you know Max? Colorful, amazing, a fine scholar though rather iconoclastic. . . . You don't know Max? I'm sure he's here; I'll introduce you. He'd be delighted to meet you, Bernadine. We correspond a great deal and we've been on panels together . . . every time we meet I say, *Max, when you complete that Woolf book, you must do some serious thinking about Bernadine Donovan!* And Max always slaps me on the back and. . . ."

The red-haired woman had wandered away, out of sight.

"The first year or so, I believe she came just to find Max," Herman said. "Literally haunting the poor man . . . of course, he can handle such problems. Now I think she comes just for the conference itself . . . she was supposed to be brilliant, a very fine A+ student . . . but if I see Max I'll alert him. Some say he deserves it all. But—! His new wife turning against him . . . and that vicious attack in the *New York Review* . . . You wouldn't know it, but he was in my graduating class at Harvard; and he looks a decade older. A ravaged face, like Auden's. But undauntable—unique."

At dinner Herman talked confidentially about his plans: the completion of several projects he was working on, the Lowell interview which could be expanded into a book, perhaps, if he could get a grant and a year's leave from teaching, and his own trifling attempts at poetry . . . yes, he was still writing! And he had arranged for a review-essay in *Minnesota Quarterly* of all five of Bernadine's novels, to be done by a young graduate student truly enamoured of Donovan. "No spiteful little side-glances, no niggardly *buts, howevers, excepts.* I promise you," he laughed. He squeezed her hand and released it. It might have been his nervousness, or because of the iced glass he kept raising to his mouth, but his flesh struck her as damp and clammy, like her own. Now that they were alone together in a fairly quiet restaurant, Herman seemed overbearing, edgily forceful. He might have been a little drunk. Bernadine had considered the prospect of marrying him—many times, she had considered it—and though she did, in a way, very much want to marry him, at the same time the abstract issue of marriage itself tormented her: so much intimacy, forever? *How could anyone endure it?*

They had nearly married, just the same. The date had been set, even, and Bernadine had literally run away—had flown to England just before the Sunday they were to visit Herman's widowed mother, who lived in a residential hotel-nursing home in White Plains. Herman had described his mother as "formidable" but "gracious"; he had assured Bernadine that they would get along beautifully. It was then that Bernadine realized she was about to become *married*. And she would acquire a *mother-in-law*. And a *husband*.

So, seven years ago that November, she had fled.

And now Herman was squeezing her hand, smiling tensely, telling her how charming she looked—her hair was much more attractive, in that style—and the light-green dress brought out the cool, startling clear green of her eyes.

"Do you know how formidable you are, Bernadine?" he asked suddenly.

There were many parties in the Palmer House that evening, most of them textbook publishers' parties in large suites, where the gatherings were noisy and promiscuous. The doors were left open; people drifted in and out; passing by the 10th-floor suite occupied by Prentice-Hall representatives, Bernadine glanced in to see a smoke-clogged room dense with people, one of them the tall, lost, white-faced girl in the poncho. Herman steered her along, avoiding a couple arguing in the corridor—the woman tearful, wiping her smudged eyes with the hem of her pull-over jersey blouse—and a young man in belted camel's hair trousers and a red shirt, who was vomiting into a sand-filled urn, groaning miserably.

The party they were going to was by invitation only, given by a New York literary quarterly for which Herman did book reviews occasionally; so he was disappointed to see the doors to that suite open as well. Bernadine held his arm, nervously. He told her not to worry—he wouldn't let people bother her. And he was very attentive to her all evening. He stayed close, leaving her side only to refill a glass from time to time. He was even a little jealous, though jokingly so, when an old classmate of Bernadine's from college hurried over to her to congratulate her on her "burgeoning reputation." He was now a professor at Yale, he told her; charmingly self-deprecatory, with graying muttonchop whiskers and prominent, keen eyes, in a handsome tweed suit with a checked vest, he asked Bernadine if she missed the old days, when the two of them had competed so happily for A's and smiles of approval from their professors. Bernadine blushed. She laughed. "Yes," he sighed, "it's entirely different to be on the other side—the giving side. I award a few A's, of course, though I'm far more fastidious than my more 'liberalized' colleagues, and I smile my approval to the deserving few. . . . But it isn't the same thing at all. It's like getting to be God, and then discovering it's no different than when you were seventeen. Or is writing somehow different?—Did you know that Hennessey died? Yes. Stroke. Right in his Renaissance non-dramatic class. We always fantasized that he might—didn't we?—so many, many years ago, how red-faced and huffing the poor dear would get!—no there just aren't scholars like Hennessey any longer. —And Paxton, did you hear? Youngish man, just joined the staff when we graduated? Paralyzed from the neck down. Had signed a contract for one of those gross California schools—half-again his salary at Harvard, his own secretary, enormous office, only one graduate course to teach—but the threat of it was too much, evidently his deeper self simply rebelled. He's been para-lyzed now for two years, they say. I must say I might react sim-ilarly—leaving the East Coast, you know—very difficult, very dif-ficult indeed. I gather from your expression that you agree, Ber-nadine?"

But Herman interrupted, leading Bernadine over to meet a stocky, perspiring woman, introduced as *the well-known* . . . and a name Bernadine didn't quite catch . . . evidently a professor somewhere in Boston. She and Bernadine shook hands enthusiastically. "I haven't read your novels—I fully intend to—everyone, truly everyone admires them so much—but I'm so overwhelmed with my special interests, my research and reviewing—I hope you'll forgive me." Herman stood between them, beaming. It turned out that the woman was an old colleague of his, a "friendly rival"; she was the well-known Ellie Sax, whose reviews so playfully criss-crossed Herman's, as he put it. "What I elevate El tries her damnedest to knock down," Herman said, "but of course it's vice-versa too, isn't

188

it Ellie?" But Ellie seemed to like Bernadine very much. She kept touching her arm, even squeezing it, as they spoke. "I think I *did* read a story of yours years ago in the *New Yorker,* a lovely little Chekhovian piece . . . perfect," Ellie said. "It's just criminal of me to have so neglected you. And now it's myself who must admit to being embarrassed, since I see there's a panel discussion of your work scheduled for tomorrow. How marvelous it must be! A kind of immortality while you're still alive! —Or do you dread it, Bernadine? I think I would."

She was slit-eyed with an emotion Bernadine could not comprehend: not anything so simple as envy or malice, but a fawning, even gushing and intimate enthusiasm, made sinister by her habit of continually licking her lips. "In the past, of course," Ellie said, "*of course* such honors were reserved only for the dead. In England, I assume . . . I assume their tradition hasn't wavered. And Mr. Philip Larkin himself, who I believe is a contemporary poet, has stated that Thomas Hardy was the last significant poet in English . . . a remarkable modesty on his part, very English, very unlike us in this part of the world. Of course—"

"She really can't help being alive, still," Herman giggled.

Another friend of Herman's, tall, big-nostriled, forlorn, with sad pouchy eyes, joined the little group, shaking Bernadine's hand reverently; he told her he'd read all four of her novels and eagerly awaited the next. "People like you are almost single-handedly holding the fort," he said, not releasing her hand. "The English tradition: calmness, clarity. Sanity. Against . . . against whatever else it is, I believe it's—"

"From across the Channel," Ellie said flatly.

"The French novel or whatever they call it—words all jumbled on a page, no chronological order, sheer madness— And yet I somehow blame Virginia Woolf for all of it—"

Bernadine was exhausted and ready to leave; but Herman was evidently enjoying the party. Others joined them. Bernadine stood in silence, holding her empty glass, wondering what would happen: if this were a novella of hers she could certainly shape it into a coherent and meaningful, though "ironic" experience . . . but she was beginning to realize that the Chicago setting was totally inappropriate . . . unworkable for her. It fell outside the scope of her imagination. All her novels and stories were set in Virginia, North Carolina, or Maryland; they were beautifully-plotted, ingeniously-woven tales of individuals in families, immense families of a type once known as *genteel*, when that word had not been an accusation. Of course Bernadine Donovan had freed herself of that claustophobic world and its values . . . but . . . she felt a sudden nostalgia for it, wishing violently that she had gone back to Cape Charles for the holidays, instead of coming to this awful city.

Ellie Sax and a willowy young man with an English accent were commenting wittily and contemptuously on the décor of the room; the sad-eyed man, who turned out to be the editor of the literary magazine giving the party, was rapidly informing Bernadine about their upcoming issues, "collectors' items," and what a pity they hadn't a Donovan story. . . . But he knew how infrequently she published; he respected her dedication to her craft. Bernadine laughed faintly, about to remind him that they had rejected a story of hers not too long ago—so hurting her, so upsetting her, that she hadn't dared show them another. . . . But Herman spoke to a passing waiter, a black man, and Bernadine stood silent. He always addressed waiters and taxi-cab drivers in an extremely amiable manner. It intrigued her, it pleased her at least at times, that he should assume so comradely a tone with them, a tone he didn't use with other people. In London, that week he had spent seven years ago pleading with her to return and marry him—she'd almost loved him, it had been so hectic and romantic a period in her life —he had sounded wonderfully American, chatting with cab-drivers and busboys and hotel clerks. *What a press of people!* he said cheerfully. *And don't envy them for an instant—if you do—there are 600'0 of us out of work, isn't that shocking?* But the willowy young man denounced that as an "exaggeration." Ellie sided with him; it was an exaggeration, certainly.

"Well, some very gloomy statistic, anyway," Herman said. The waiter slipped away; Bernadine was going to suggest that they leave. But she saw a face, suddenly, that was familiar to her—

Martin Stanley—a handsome, bald critic in his late fifties, elegantly dressed for the party in a dark blue three-piece suit, with a dark blue tie. Two years ago, when he had interviewed her, he had been glamorously youthful, his sideburns wild and curly, his outfit a kind of costume, all stripes and zigzags. Ellie Sax hurried over to him, plump, beaming; she seized his arm and they fell into an animated conversation. Bernadine blushed, hoping Stanley would not notice her. She certainly didn't want to talk to him.

Stanley had "done" a number of contemporary writers, and Bernadine had reluctantly, very reluctantly, agreed to his many pleas that she be included in the study: *You're too important to be omitted!* It had taken place nearly two years ago, but Bernadine remembered it all so clearly. . . . Courteous, excessively attentive, Martin Stanley had recorded their conversation on tape and had also taken notes; he had listened to her every syllable. Then he left, returned to his own apartment a few blocks from Bernadine's, in the East 50's, and made up a completely different interview: a few remarks were kept, but most of the dialogue, and certainly Bernadine's person, itself, were all changed. She had read the piece when it came out, in a popular intellectual weekly, and could not believe it. She really could not believe it. He had described her subdued, tasteful four-room apartment as "carelessly and confidently Bohemian, Aging Avant-Garde"; Bernadine herself had been described as possessing that "good-natured, husky, humorless swagger of the small woman." The essay's concluding paragraph had spoken of her as one of *the* finest of living American women writers, though she "had not yet located her true subject or a style in which to express it."

She hated and feared him.

Fortunately, he now wanted to escape from Ellie Sax, and was backing away. Ellie tried to follow him, gave up, and wandered over to the hors d'oeuvre table, where she absent-mindedly began eating. Bernadine was so upset by the presence of Martin Stanley that for a while she simply watched Ellie, without noticing how hungrily and yet mechanically she ate. Hand over hand, tiny sandwiches with pale greeny paste, smoked salmon on crackers, with

191

curlicues of black olives pressed in place . . . her mouth and the clinging bosom of her dress flaked with crumbs. . . . Her profile, emphasizing the bulge of her chin, was at once aristocratic and piggish: a remarkable woman! She strolled along the length of the table, eating, and licking her lips, and discovered a martini glass someone had abandoned, with an inch or so of liquid in it. She lifted it to her lips and sipped it. And at that moment she happened to glance around: she saw Bernadine watching her.

Immediately her eyes became slits.

Bernadine thought, panicked: *That woman will be my enemy forever.*

Herman ordered champagne from Room Service, "to celebrate."

"Celebrate?"

"The seventh year of our not being married."

He was pink-skinned now from all the conversations, his tie loosened, his jacket off. With a long loose wavering sigh he said, playfully, rakishly, something about next year: what would next year be?

They were sitting in brush-velvet chairs, in Bernadine's room, facing each other over a coffee table; Bernadine was fidgeting with her watch, since she was unaccustomed to wearing jewelry of any kind, and yet she did not dare take the watch off—it might strike Herman as an intimate gesture, a symbolic move. She drank champagne, quickly. Herman sighed again and lapsed into a recounting of the people he had talked with that evening . . . summarizing them all, with brisk jarring barks of laughter. The Sax creature, divorced years ago from a dear friend of his named Henderson: quite merciless, really, stole from her graduate students, as everyone knew, but remarkable—formidable—extremely high standards. That friend of Bernadine's from Yale—did she know about *him?*

"I—"

He began a complicated story, punctuated by laughter, which seemed to deal with the man's inability to come to grips with his

192

"sexual identity" . . . though Bernadine was so tired, now, she hardly listened. It was good to be with him, however. Her apartment in New York was so lonely at times, so empty. . . . If they were married he would chat like this, happily, wittily, with that impersonal sweeping irony that carried all before it . . . and he knew so much, he seemed to know everyone there was to know, while Bernadine had become almost a recluse since the shock of the Martin Stanley "interview." She was briskly efficient, even a trifle mannish, in her own way, but shy at times, hideously self-conscious, and perhaps Herman Geller could help her. . . . It was not too late: she wasn't yet forty, and Herman was no more than forty-five.

Suddenly, glumly, he mentioned some stray news—"good" news—Max Lippe had been given the Chair of American Studies at Leeds, England, which was why he wasn't attending this year's convention.

"Max is my age," he said, with a sigh like a thud. ". . . But he looks at least ten years older." He turned the champagne glass in his fingers, then finished what remained in it; without looking at Bernadine he said in a lowered voice, "I want to marry you."

Bernadine could not speak.

"The letters I send you aren't really the ones I write . . . I write long desperate letters, then throw them away. . . . I feel that I . . . we . . . it would be so good, so perfect. . . . If. . . . I don't suppose you happened to read those poems of mine, recently published in *Aardvark*? No, I didn't think so. No. Yet they were written for you. They were written for you."

Bernadine was very moved. She tried to explain that she never saw that particular magazine—wasn't familiar with it—

Herman rose, wiping his damp face with a cocktail napkin.

"I understand," he said sadly. "Well, we can discuss it another time, we have lots of time."

"I'm so sorry— But I— I—"

"If rumors have come your way, rumors about me and—and anyone else—ugly vicious rumors spread by a vindictive set of persons— If they've already poisoned you against me, and caused you to doubt me—" He looked at her, adjusting his glasses nervously. "That isn't it, is it?"

But Bernadine had heard no rumors; she walked with him to the door, eager to console him. They were both very tired, she said, and it was no time to discuss such important matters. They must both get a good night's sleep. There was no question of his staying in this room, evidently, which was a relief to Bernadine, and perhaps to Herman as well. He hoped she would enjoy the panel discussion of her work—unfortunately he couldn't attend it, since he had scheduled a breakfast meeting with Douglas MacKendrick, the new, aggressive young editor of an East Coast review, and he hoped she would understand—

That was a relief to her too.

Though she was by no means old-fashioned, and really very "liberated" from her background and its narrow rules of conduct, still Bernadine had never exactly had a lover; somehow it had not happened. It had nearly happened with Herman, several times. But finally it had not happened. Once, in her early thirties, she had isolated the problem, tracing it to her characteristic meticulousness, her need to pre-arrange, pre-imagine, pre-structure everything. It seemed to her only civilized that one must proceed through a series of drafts, before plunging into reality. And so she had never managed to lose her viriginity, though she had known Herman for eighteen years and, in a strange way, they were perhaps married . . . mutual acquaintances often seemed to assume they were married, though not living together for some reason. It was all very awkward, yet it made a kind of sense.

It was love of a physical type that seemed to her mysterious: not ugly or vulgar or even untidy, but simply impossible. At times she seriously doubted whether *anyone* really did such things. . . . Perhaps it was all pretense? Or a literary convention?

Bernadine had registered at the conference as *B. G. Sullivan,* of New York City; that was all her plastic badge showed. Everyone else seemed to be affiliated with a college or university. In the morning she stood a few doors away from the Cameo Room, watching to see who was going in to the Donovan panel . . . absurdly excited, girlish, at the same time knowing how vain she was being . . . how humiliated if someone found her out. *Bernadine Donovan! You!* But she saw no one she knew. The men and women strolling along this corridor were all strangers; no one from the party of the evening before was going to attend her panel, evidently; of course, it was one of the 11 A.M. sections, and that was fairly early . . . especially if the party had lasted a while. She leafed through the program and discovered that the Donovan panel faced harsh competition: a panel of three distinguished Chaucerian scholars were discussing final *e's* in Chaucer, in the Rotunda; Professor Maddox of Cambridge was addressing a group in the Small Ballroom, on the subject of Norse influences upon pre-Shakespearean drama; and in the Grand Ballroom, at the end of this very corridor, a panel consisting of Martin Stanley and two other well-known critics was discussing "Black Humor and Psychosis." Bernadine couldn't help noticing how people were drifing into the Grand Ballroom. . . .

A young man with an attaché case and a badge that proclaimed NYU hurried into the Donovan room; then, to Bernadine's dismay, backed out again and went down the hall to the Grand Ballroom. It was nearly 11 o'clock now. But people were wandering in: *Jolene Snyder* of *Milwaukee Community College . . . Bobbie Rae Dean* of *Lamar Tech . . . Rodney Wong* of *St. Clair Extension.* When *D. J. Fox* of *Princeton* and *E. Cleary* of *Columbia* appeared, well-dressed and a trifle bleary-eyed from partying the night before, Bernadine was saddened but not surprised to see them bypass the Cameo Room and hurry into the Grand Ballroom. Several young men, looking hardly out of their twenties, strode by, one of them bumping into Bernadine. She overheard them mention a rumor—well, maybe it wasn't a rumor!—that Vonnegut himself would show up at the panel, in a disguise—

The Donovan session began at 11:08. There were about thirty-five people there, for which Bernadine was grateful—what if no

195

one had showed up at all? She sat at the very back, near the door. That morning she had fluffed out her hair and put on lipstick, which she rarely wore; she was even wearing her clear-rimmed reading glasses. But there seemed no danger of anyone recognizing her . . . no one was even looking at her. Just as the session was opening, with several halting, breathless remarks by a middle-aged woman Bernadine had thought to be a nurse, seeing her earlier, but who was in fact *Sister Bridget* of *St. Anne's College, N.H.*, a trousered girl in her twenties slipped into a seat beside Bernadine. The girl immediately opened a notebook and began writing in it, furiously.

Bernadine had not really been nervous until now. But Sister Bridget spoke so faintly . . . *So happy to see you all . . . so glad you could all attend . . . a very very important date in American letters . . . first serious critical attention paid to . . . to. . . .* The woman wore a navy blue dress, pragmatic and somehow very sad; her hair, exposed, was wispily brown; her voice kept faltering, as she adjusted the hand microphone several times. She and three others sat behind a narrow table, on a platform raised about six inches from the floor. There was only one man on the panel, a thin, downlooking young man named Erich Larson, from a small community college in New Rochelle.

The first paper dealt with "The Influence of Woolf's Mature Style on the Fiction of Bernadine Donovan."

. . . Mr. Larson was reading his paper so rapidly and breathlessly that he was well into it by the time Sister Bridget asked him to speak more clearly; he glared up at the audience, clutching his notes. But he forced himself to read more slowly. Bernadine must have been in a daze, because it took her a while to realize that the thesis of the paper was a very upsetting one: Donovan, *one of our finest living stylists*, was evidently so deeply indebted to Virginia Woolf that, *in a manner of speaking*, she could be considered a development of Woolf rather than an independent artist. . . . Mr. Larson swallowed; he paused to take a breath. He told the audience, spontaneously, that Bernadine Donovan was by far *his favorite living writer*—there were a few isolated claps at this—but at the same time he had to admit, after having done an exhaustive study of Donovan's prose style, that the parallels were so obvious as to be at times embarrassing.

To prove his thesis, he read a number of paragraphs from *The Years* juxtaposed with paragraphs from Bernadine's most recent novel, *Symmetries.* He read rapidly, stammering from time to time. Yet his voice was eager and dramatic. He stressed certain words and phrases time and again—*the line of trees, the mist, the horizon, the bright sunshine*—until Bernadine herself could not have said which was which. . . . She had not read *The Years* since the age of eighteen. It was absurd, Mr. Larson's thesis. Yet people were taking notes . . . Sister Bridget and another nun were taping the session. . . .

But—!

After Mr. Larson finished his paper there was a brief discussion between the panelists and several people at the front of the room: whether the Woolfian influence was valid only for *Symmetries*, or for all of Donovan's work. Or might it be (a proposal suggested impishly by a man in a beret) really Proust who was behind them both? This led into a discussion of "male," "female" and "androgynous" literary styles and whether there was any difference between them.

Bernadine took a handkerchief out of her purse and dabbed at her eyes. . . . So hurt. So insulted. . . . And no one defended her. . . . Beside her, the girl continued to scribble away in her notebook; she must have been writing a letter.

The next paper was called "Angst and Irony in Donovan"—an attempt to show how Donovan's "terse bitter language" contradicted the overt "plot-structured" work itself; the conclusion being that the novels' *real messages* were in each case *antithetical* to what was stated. The woman—an Assistant Professor at San Diego State—read her paper without pause, quoting a number of reviewers and critics at great length, contemptuously, pointing out how every one of them had erred. The most ignominious of all was one Herman Geller, writing in *Minnesota Quarterly:* he spoke of Donovan's celebration of order and hope for redemption, when it was obvious that Donovan meant nothing of the sort, that her devilishly clever little novels were celebrations of nihilism . . . dark rejoicings over the fact that *civilization as we know it is finished.*

After this paper only a few people argued; the man in the beret left by a side door.

The final paper, "Donovan and Swift," was read in a slow, dreamy Southern voice by Edna Corrington, a woman who described herself as a devoted reader of Bernadine Donovan . . . a *devoted* critic . . . lately reduced to somewhat amateurish status since she had been "let go" (a euphemism) at Atlanta State College. But she was not bitter, not at all. She was very pleased to be here. Very proud to have been invited by the Modern Language Association to read a paper before a group of distinguished scholars and critics. . . . The paper seemed to be mostly lists and catalogues of images, with an emphasis upon birds, airplanes, holes in the ground, and the "thingness" of things. *Symmetries,* it was gradually revealed, had been modelled not upon *The Years* but upon the first three books of *Gulliver's Travels.* All of the scatological references had been transposed into images of food or cooking, a most delicious irony, as the woman put it, since *Symmetries* was—on its very surface— a novel concerned with an old Virgina family. And—

Bernadine sat with her arms tightly folded across her chest. Her gaze lowered, her lashes trembling on the brink of tears, she forbade herself any agitation; she was not going to break. But suddenly there was a question raised—or a shout—and then someone was standing in the first row— Right before the dais someone was shouting for them to stop.

"You stop! Stop! —Oh, you *stop* that! I know who you are!"

It was the red-haired woman, in the same outfit she had worn the day before. She had jumped to her feet, astonishing everyone. Sister Bridget tried to quiet her, but she stepped up onto the platform and turned to face the group, her bony shoulder raised coquettishly, her frizzy red hair wild about her face. "All of you—I know who you are! *I know!* You're lying about me, aren't you— lying about me, Bernadine Donovan—all of you telling nasty filthy lies about me—*about me*—"

Suddenly she lost her courage. She looked around, as if not knowing how she had gotten there. A man came quickly forward to help her up the aisle . . . she walked with him, submissively, though as she was about to leave she giggled and cried out something about "signing autographs in the lobby."

Then it was over.

Everyone was out in the aisle, asking what had happened. Had that been . . . ? *Had that really been* . . . ? At the front of the room, Sister Bridget tried to call them back to order, but it was hopeless. The girl beside Bernadine got to her feet, slowly. She said to Bernadine, "Wow Jesus, she *did* show up. There was a rumor about her and Vonnegut. *Wow*. And stoned to the gills. What a historic event—what's-her-name completely stoned-out!"

Bernadine got to her feet shakily. People were standing around, milling around in the aisle . . . the girl got away before Bernadine could seize her arm and explain . . . explain that the mad-woman had not been Donovan . . . a mistake, a terrible mistake . . . tragic mistake. . . . *How sad!* someone was marveling. *How horrible! . . . Was that really Donovan herself? No! Yes!* Bernadine staggered toward someone who was arguing that that mad-woman was *not* Miss Donovan: never! *Bernadine is a very short squattish woman and much older than that nut!* But now people were leaving. Everyone was leaving. A white-haired gentleman from Florida State tried to get by Bernadine, but she seized his arm and said, "Sir, please —wait— *I'm Bernadine Donovan!* Please—" He glanced at her name-tag, smiled fearfully, and elbowed her aside to escape. She tried to stop several nuns, dressed in old-fashioned habits, but they eluded her and left by the side door.

Bernadine snatched off her badge and hurried to the dais.

The woman whose paper had been interrupted was arguing with Sister Bridget. "It isn't fair! A thing like this! Interrupting my paper! This was my only chance—my last chance—I demand financial restitution—I won't accept this, do you hear! Costing me hundreds and hundreds of dollars, this dreadful convention—this Donovan thing was my ace in the hole—"

Bernadine was about to reveal herself to them—but the look in Sister Bridget's eyes, a squeezed-in jerky terror, decided her against it.

She left.

She wandered for a while along the mezzanine, running her hand on the brass railing. Occasionally people from the Donovan section would pass her, marveling about what had happened . . . *It certainly was her! Looked just like her! . . . No! . . . Yes! . . .* but she paid them no attention, now. She walked aimlessly, staggering as if exhausted. Well. The papers had been read, the panel was over. Yes. She had ventured out to Chicago, and. Yes. It had happened. Something had happened. Had happened.

. . . She found herself gazing down into the crowded lobby, past the tinsel and angel-fluff of the giant Christmas tree. She could see that group of nuns . . . winding their way through the lobby, getting stuck in a *cul de sac* . . . backing out, heading bravely onward. . . . She leaned against the polished railing, staring. Time must have passed. Into her vision, careening into focus, was a man who resembled Herman . . . yes, Herman Geller, her husband. He was far to the side of the lobby, out of the stream of people, leaning against a marble pillar and chatting with a bellboy, a young dusky-skinned lad his own height. They were laughing about something, Herman most heartily of all; he flung both arms back in a spontaneous gesture Bernadine had never seen him make before. . . .

The vision faded. Wobbled. Blurred. . . . Perhaps she was looking for the mad-woman, down there in the crowd. But no, really she was looking for no one. She leaned over the railing, in a kind of peace. After a while she roused herself, as if calling her soul back into her body. It was reluctant to come back: it resisted. But she roused herself, she woke, and called it back.

And it did come back, gradually.

(October 1973)

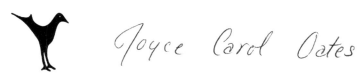*Joyce Carol Oates*

Printed March-April 1974 in Santa Barbara & Ann Arbor for the Black Sparrow Press by Noel Young & Edwards Brothers Inc. Design by Barbara Martin. This first edition is published in paper wrappers; there are 1000 hardcover copies; & 350 copies handbound in boards by Earle Gray which are numbered & signed by the author.

242

JOYCE CAROL OATES was born in 1938 and grew up in the country outside Lockport, New York. She was graduated from Syracuse University in 1960 and received her Master's degree in English from the University of Wisconsin.

From the start of her writing career Ms. Oates has earned high literary acclaim. She was awarded a Guggenheim Fellowship in 1967-68 and the Richard and Hinda Rosenthal Foundation Award of the National Institute of Arts and Letters for her novel *A Garden of Earthly Delights* (1967). Her novel, *them*, won the National Book Award for Fiction in 1970. *The Wheel of Love* (1970) contains many prize-winning stories. Her most recent novel, published in the fall of 1973, was called *Do With Me What You Will.* In the fall of 1973 Black Sparrow Press published *The Hostile Sun: the Poetry of D. H. Lawrence,* and in the fall of 1974 will publish a new work entitled *Miracle Play.*

Ms. Oates is Professor of English at the University of Windsor ın Ontario.